Love Wasn't the Goal

A SURPRISE PREGNANCY ROMANCE

J. NICHOLE

not the last page

This book was written before SCOTUS reversed Roe v. Wade, and as I became outraged over the news, I realized this book was coming.

This book illustrates a woman's choice to decide what is best for her.

I hope you agree that a woman should maintain every right to decide what is best for her.

J. Nichole Newsletter

I'd love to keep in touch with you, and if you feel the same, join my newsletter.

By the way, for joining, I'll send you a free book!

https://mailchi.mp/notthelastpage/ebook

Chapter One

Nico

  Sitting in a hospital room, ass cheeks out, wasn't the way I liked to spend my day. But I had become accustomed to my annual check-up. For ten years straight I had to visit this cardiologist to ensure my heart was still pumping the way it should and no further symptoms were occurring. Being that I was able to sit there, and stare at the diagrams of hearts on the wall, was a good indication that I hadn't succumbed to my diagnosis.

  Ten years ago, I wouldn't have thought I'd be able to say the same. That day on the basketball court when I fainted—felt a light shining in my eyes—I just knew I was about to greet the Lord, but had no idea what I would say or if I was ready, yet. Later, I found out the light shining was just the paramedic checking my vitals before wheeling me off to the waiting ambulance. The Lord wasn't ready for me, thank God.

  I laughed to myself as I waited, because Dr. Wilson was never on time, including today. My legs were dangling over the table, my clothes tossed on the chair beside me. I had glanced at the clock at least five times already, and it seemed that only five minutes had passed. I was growing impatient because the weekend was calling me—and Dr. Wilson was the only barrier between me answering.

I heard a light tap on the door, before he walked in. "Doc," I said with a smile, "Nice for you to join me."

He laughed and patted my back. "Nico, it's always a pleasure to see you." The short Black man, with a full head of grey hair, wrinkled skin, and a beard closely shaved, had aged over the years. I was thankful to have consistent care because I could skip the formalities and get to the good stuff. "How are you feeling?"

Except I couldn't just give him a generic response. "Still breathing." My smile went crooked. "So I guess pretty damn good."

He shook his head. "Nico, Nico."

When I was first diagnosed with hypertrophic cardiomyopathy it was not only a lesson in sounding out medical terms, but a lesson in learning the symptoms, and the long-term impacts of the diagnosis, which was the kicker. I wasn't just on the court playing my heart out that day, I was playing for the scouts, my Division One scholarship was already concrete, but I had a few other schools who were interested in me. I was playing for the opportunity to dominate at the next level.

When Dr. Wilson and I first met, it wasn't exactly on the best of terms. I may, or may not, have had a few choice words shouted at the four walls while he was in my presence. I had to eventually realize it wasn't him who gave me the disease—but learning who did was the other blow I wasn't ready for.

During all that learning, I realized it was a genetic disease carried by my mother, passed on to her favorite son. The fucking irony.

Although the diagnosis didn't have to end my basketball career, my symptoms proved to be a challenge to manage. Therefore, my dreams of playing ball quickly came to an end. The colleges who were all after me were no longer interested, that Division One scholarship that was prominently offered was withdrawn with their *sincerest apologies for my diagnosis.*

Being able to tell Dr. Wilson, "I'm pretty damn good," was a highlight in our ten-year relationship. Because honestly, it took me some time to get there. My diagnosis, and subsequent end of my basketball career, came with months of anger, followed by sadness. Those who knew me back then likely found me to be quite the asshole. Including Dr. Wilson, at least that's what he told me years later.

"Any tightness in your chest, shortness of breath, trouble when you are active?"

I repeated, "Active," followed by a hearty laugh. "Naw, Doc, I haven't been experiencing any of that."

He took notes on his tablet, remaining silent as he did. When he finally looked up he was coming toward me with his stethoscope outstretched. "Alright, let me take a listen." He instructed, "Deep breath in," as he moved it around my chest, and then my back. "Sounds like your heart." Which probably meant he could hear the irregularity that had become infamous.

"Good, glad it's still in there." I bragged, "Was thinking about going skydiving, think it'll make it?"

Dr. Wilson crossed his arms across his chest. "Still out here trying to defy death, huh?" I shrugged. "If you answer the questionnaire truthfully, it's likely they wouldn't let you proceed anyway."

I groaned. "Ah, discrimination at its finest. Here I was thinking being a Black man in America had its difficulties." I shook my head. "A Black man with a heart disease, damn. More ways to hold me back," I joked.

"Glad to see you in good spirits, Nico," Dr. Wilson told me

as he headed to the door. "Don't do anything that will test the limits of your heart, got it?"

My lips tightened and I didn't make any promises. Like Dr. Wilson said, since my diagnosis, that was the one thing I promised myself, I'd live fully. The disease had taken away enough. I deserved to be out there living it up, making up for what was lost.

At least that's what I told myself. I figured after a life-altering diagnosis, I had two options. Retreat, and live life carefully, afraid of what could happen next. Or bounce back, better than I was before. There was a third, less interesting option, make sure my legacy lived on through my seed. I called that one the Nick Cannon option, and because I wasn't the fatherly type, that option was off the table for me. I was good with the favorite uncle title, at most.

I hopped down from the exam table, bundled up the bare-all hospital gown, and used my shooting arm to shoot it into the bin beside me. Once I was dressed, and exiting the doctor's office—helmet in hand—I was ready to hit up the nearest bar for a toast, to ten years of living.

The streets of Atlanta weren't easy to navigate during rush hour, but on the back of my all-black Suzuki GSX-R1000, I was weaving in and out of cars, zipping past the standstill. Pulling up to The Establishment, I made sure the few ladies walking in heard my engine rev before I parked nearby.

A couple of years ago, I picked up another daring adventure. I started riding a bike, and hadn't stopped. The adrenaline rush as the wind whipped past me gave me that feeling that I was dribbling the ball down the court, ready to shoot, as I watched everyone in awe of my athletic abilities.

Maybe it was, "Risking it," as my mama tried to tell me. Not the safest way I could spend, "my second chance." But what good was a second chance if I tiptoed through life as if it couldn't be taken from me in a blink? I remembered that as I strolled into the bar, on the lookout for Hendrix, and eyeing any women that could have been my adventure for the night.

"Yo," I yelled as I walked up to the bar. Hendrix was in the middle of his order to the bartender when I told him, "Let me grab an Old Fashioned." I leaned against the bar and looked around—happy hour was packed. I looked down the bar and saw the ladies who were walking in when I pulled up. One, with dreads down her back, was looking my way. "Damn, bruh," I whispered to Hendrix as he handed me a drink. "I may go down and chat with ol' girl."

He looked down the bar, in her direction, then smiled back at me. "Do you, bruh." He smirked. "What better way to celebrate than to have someone to take home with you tonight?"

"C'mon," I told him, "You're still single, right?" Hendrix and I had been friends since high school. We balled on the same court, both of us breaking school records, attracting scouts from the best schools. When my career ended, his continued. He had lived the dream I always imagined—college ball, drafted into the NBA, but now he was back, retired, and running a car dealership. In all that time, all the chicks likely throwing themselves at him, he stayed single. At times.

"Yeah man," he sighed as if being single was a bad thing. "Let's go." He nodded in their direction.

Before either of us could speak, the ladies looked up to us and one mentioned, "Were you the one on the bike?" after noticing my helmet in my arm. I nodded and rested it on the floor in front of me. "And you," she narrowed her eyes, "are you Hendrix Moore?" Hendrix nodded his head, the usual smile that lit up his face didn't appear. A sign that he was really in his feelings about his latest breakup.

"I'm Nico." I held out my free hand. "You?" She told me her name was Lizzie. Her friend introduced herself, keeping her eye on Hendrix. "Nice to meet you, Lizzie."

Lizzie cozied into my side, asking questions about my bike, questions that let me know she was very familiar. "At one point in time I was going to buy one." She smiled softly before telling me, "But talked myself out of it."

"If you are ever interested in riding, I got you." Her eyes widened. "In fact," I told her, "Where are you headed after this?"

She looked over at her friend before responding, "I was probably headed back to my place." Then she quickly added, "But we just met, I probably shouldn't hop on the back of your bike." Her nose scrunched up.

I wagged my head. "You're probably right." Instead of riding down the highway, we stayed at the bar, all of us getting better acquainted.

I learned that she was a teacher, and the stories she told about her second graders concreted my desire to stay in the uncle lane. "One kid has this thing with jumping out of his seat every couple of hours," she laughed, "just dancing for no damn reason." Then she added, "It's irritating, but I must admit the shit is funny." She laughed. "Most days I can ignore it and keep teaching. Some days I have to bite my tongue to keep from laughing."

"Are all the kids as lively?" I asked.

With her hand tapping the rim of her glass, she told me, "You know, they are all unique, but not all of them bounce off the walls *all day.*"

"Enough of me." She fanned her hand toward me. "Tell me more about you." Her eyes scanned from my feet, up my body till they reached my eyes again. "Do you play ball too?" My sheer height alone, six foot five, often elicited the same exact question too often.

I looked behind me to Hendrix, still talking with her friend. At Lizzie, I shook my head. "No, I played in high school."

"Were you any good?" That question reminded me of my days on the court. The twenty points I could easily put on the board each game. When I explained, staying humble, Hendrix spoke up from beside me.

"This guy right here was a legend." He smiled at Lizzie. "One of the best players coming out of Georgia."

"Coming from the guy who played years in the NBA." I laughed.

Lizzie's eyes narrowed and she asked, "Who was better?" Neither me nor Hendrix responded. We competed during practice, played hard during the game, I cheered for him during each of his college and NBA games. When I fainted, then got the diagnosis, Hendrix was the one who visited the most. He didn't try to tell me everything would be okay. He loved basketball as much as I did and he knew playing professionally was all either of us wanted to do.

"You are both modest." Lizzie smiled then winked at her friend. "I like that." Then she slid her cup across the bar toward the bartender before she told me, "I think I'll take you up on that ride."

"Good," I told her. As we walked down the street to my bike, I thought skydiving would have been exhilarating, but as Lizzie wrapped her arms around my waist, I thought, *I'd rather die fucking than jumping out of a plane anyway.*

Chapter Two

Destiny

What could be more beautiful than a bride on her wedding day? The lace, the tulle, the makeup, the genuine smile—it was like sunshine was bursting from each limb of Monroe's body. She was gorgeous, and I couldn't be more excited to be her bridesmaid. I took my job seriously—she needed her dress fluffed? I was on it. If she needed a tea to calm her throat after our wild night out, I made sure she had enough cream and sugar. If her tears were flowing, and she needed a few reassuring words to remind her that the love of her life was waiting at the end of the aisle, my words were poetic.

I did all that because I could only hope, when it was time for me and Jensen to walk down the aisle, she'd do the same for me.

Monroe's day was magical—the weather a perfect seventy-five degrees, the sun was shining, the birds were chirping. None of the groomsmen skipped a beat as they escorted us down the aisle. Monroe and Alex's vows were personally written, and when read there was not a single dry eye in the building. Well, except for Jensen. Our eyes connected, and as I dabbled at the tears streaming down my face, I noticed him shifting uncomfortably.

The "I love you" I mouthed that he seemingly ignored had me thinking there was something going on with him. I didn't think anything of it. Instead, I danced with the groomsmen back up the aisle after the lovely couple was introduced as husband and wife. There was the bridesmaid dance, then, of course, my carefully written, well-rehearsed speech, then finally we were able to relax. Seated next to Jensen, I went on and on about the details Monroe's wedding planner did not miss. "Did you see the framed pictures of them as kids?" I asked, quickly proceeding with, "Think your mom has a cute one of you in a tux, or maybe a suit?" He adjusted the collar of his shirt and took another bite of his steak.

"This food," I told him, "is bomb," as I took a spoonful of the creamy mashed potatoes with the extra hint of garlic.

"Yeah," he finally mumbled. "It's good."

Jensen and I had been together for two years. Meeting randomly at a networking event at a local restaurant. It didn't take long for us to hit it off. After the fourth date, we were talking long-term goals—moving in together, marriage, kids, all that shit.

Being the Maid of Honor did come with a shit ton of responsibility, though, and I thought he had been acting funky because I hadn't been around as much for the past couple of months. I was thinking he would feel much more at ease at the wedding, like finally, he'd have his girl back. I told him, "Let's dance," when I heard one of my favorite songs drop, and he hesitated. "Jensen," I asked, "you good?"

His brown eyes were sunken, his hand rubbing across his freshly edged beard. Then he admitted, "Think I'm ready to go, actually." The party had just started. Although the hardest part of the day was over, I couldn't just abandon Monroe and leave the reception early. "Think one of the bridesmaids can drop you off?"

My head tilted and my eyes narrowed as I watched him stand from his seat. "Are you serious?" He nodded his head. "Alright, yeah." Then I told him, "I'm sure one of them can bring me home." He kissed the top of my head and walked toward the exit —with me watching his tall, athletic build stroll across the room.

Monroe and Antonio were walking around the room greeting everyone. When Monroe stopped beside me, she leaned down and whispered, "A bitch has to pee," before her eyes pleaded with me.

"I got you." Her beautiful dress was adorned with a buttoned corset and a huge fluffy skirt. The only way she was going to the bathroom was with assistance. As we walked to the back of the building, she asked if Jensen was having a good time. I didn't want to ruin her night, so I kept it casual when I told her, "Oh, he actually left out."

I thought it was casual until she stopped walking and looked at me. "Left? Already?" I nodded my head. "Hmm, what's that all about?"

"Nothing for you to worry about." I looped my arm through hers. "I'm not thinking about that right now."

"*Okay*," she said as we continued walking to the bridal suite. Inside the bathroom stall, I held up her skirt around her shoulders as she eased down to the toilet. "Glad you didn't leave."

I assured her, "No way in hell I was leaving early. Not after all the work we've put in. Bitch, it's time to celebrate." We both laughed.

I wasn't lying about not worrying about Jensen's departure. When we made it back to the reception, I walked straight onto the dance floor and danced amongst the bridesmaids, some of Monroe's family, and even the groomsmen who had let loose.

When Jensen hadn't shown up to the dancefloor after a few songs, the dateless groomsman who had walked me down the aisle made note, "I thought you had a date tonight?" During the rehearsal he had flirted a little, but I let him know I wasn't an option, and warned him that Jensen would be in attendance for the wedding—just in case he decided to say something slick with him nearby.

"I did," I answered simply.

He looked over my shoulder. "Oh, he doesn't dance?" I didn't know how to tell him he had already left, so I just shook my head. "Would he mind?" He grabbed my hand as the rhythm slowed.

"I don't think he would," I told him as I left enough space between us.

"If you weren't already committed to a man who doesn't join his woman on the floor, I would have asked for your number. Taken you out to dinner, drinks, something like that."

I released his hand and told him, "I appreciate it, Thaddeus," I looked over my shoulder, "but I should go check on Monroe." His eyebrow raised, and his tongue went out across his lip as I turned to find Monroe in the sea of people.

Monroe and Alex went to the extreme for their wedding, inviting over three hundred people. Fortunately, for them, Monroe's parents took the *bride's family pays for the wedding* seriously. Her mom shared they had been saving for her wedding as much as they were saving for her college tuition.

I hadn't had the discussion with my mom about a wedding budget—because for college she could only support minimally, I doubted she had even considered supporting my wedding. She was a successful attorney, but as a single mom, she always reminded me things were a little harder.

"Destiny." I felt a soft hand touch my shoulder, and I turned to see one of the bridesmaids. "Monroe's ready to do the bouquet toss," Alexis beamed. Then she told me, "Although I know I'm catching it, we should gather everyone to the dancefloor."

Up until that point, catching the bouquet had been top of mind for me. I imagined it being like the final confirmation that Jensen and I would be well on our way down the aisle next. I looked toward Alexis and warned, "Don't get your hopes up," as I walked around the hall to gather the other single ladies.

On the floor, all of us were lined up and laughing, some of us ready to throw elbows to anyone in our way of the coveted bouquet. The DJ had Beyoncé's "Single Ladies" playing, and he was shit talking up until the, "now put your hands up," verse, and that's when Monroe threw the bouquet. The beautifully silk-bound bouquet of calla lilies went flying out of her hand, and I watched it coming toward me. My hand went up to grab it, and just as my finger grazed one of the flowers, it was snatched out of my hand. It wasn't Alexis who had it clutched to her chest either, it was one of Monroe's older aunties, one who had been married a time or two before. My mouth twisted and I rolled my eyes as I left the dancefloor angry.

The night wasn't going anything like I had planned.

My emotions were tampered, though, because I had a job to do. The rest of the night went on without a hitch. The DJ was playing the last song of the evening and had announced, "The bride and groom would like you all to join them outside as they prepare to ride off together."

I was in the bridal suite when we heard the message. "I hope the two of you have the best of time on your honeymoon," I told

Monroe as we helped her out of her wedding dress and into a white cocktail dress.

"Me too." She winked before announcing, "Ladies," her smile was accompanied with her hands to her heart, "I could not have pulled any of this off without you." She hugged us each, stopping to tell me, "Destiny, I can't wait till it's your turn."

I squeezed her a little tighter before releasing her. "Alex is waiting on his bride," I gushed.

All their guests were lined up outside of the reception hall, an all-black Maserati was parked waiting for them. Instead of throwing rice their way, we held sparklers as they ran off to the waiting car.

Before everyone scattered to their own cars, I found Alexis and asked, "Mind dropping me off at my place?" She frowned and looked over my shoulder. "I'll tell you about it in the car," I told her as I shook my head.

Alexis and her boyfriend, Phil, climbed into his truck and I got into the backseat. I was looking out of the window when Alexis turned around in her seat to ask, "Ma'am, why are we giving you a ride home?" I looked to the front of the car and saw Phil's eyes in the rearview mirror.

Sighing, I revealed, "Jensen wanted to leave early."

Alexis scoffed, "What?" Then she asked, "Did he have somewhere else to be?"

Not many of my friends were fond of Jensen, but over the two years we had been together they had learned to tolerate him. Their main gripe was that he didn't seem genuine. I could never see what they were saying and urged them to get to know him better. But it was nights like these they'd remind me that he wasn't trying to get to know them better.

As Phil drove toward my apartment, I replied, "Not to my knowledge. He probably just went home."

Alexis had turned her body enough to look at me. "And that's okay with you?" I didn't respond. "Babe." She looked at Phil. "Would there be any reason for you to have left early tonight?" She cocked her head and waited on his answer.

"I mean," he dragged, "not a good reason. But I'm cool with Alex and Monroe, so maybe it's different." Phil had no problem with our group of homegirls, he'd often join us at happy hour, and didn't mind when Alexis hosted game nights at their place. He and Jensen weren't even comparable.

"Maybe," I mumbled. The closer we got to my apartment the more I didn't want to face what was waiting on me there. I had to have a conversation with Jensen to find out what the hell happened. I needed to know why he had been in a foul mood for months. As I climbed out of the car I told Alexis, "I'll call you tomorrow."

The walk to our apartment wasn't as long as I had hoped. I was trying to rehearse how I would start the conversation. What exactly I would say when I saw him. How I'd respond if I didn't think his explanation was acceptable. Then I opened the front door of the apartment and saw luggage.

Jensen, dressed in sweatpants and a t-shirt, walked out of the bedroom and paused in the middle of the living room. "Going somewhere?" I asked, pointing toward the suitcases.

The words left his mouth poignantly, and although I heard what he said, I asked him to repeat himself anyway. "I'm leaving. I don't want this anymore." The second time hearing the words didn't sound as heartfelt as the first. They felt stale, stagnant, cold. My hand went to my mouth, my eyes narrowed. "I don't want to be married." I waited for him to tell me he didn't want to be married at all, but the gut punch came when he whispered, "To you."

My head tilted to the side. "You don't want to be married." I blinked slowly. "To me?" Everything he was saying was coming out of nowhere—it seemed. Other than him being in a funky mood, we had hardly had any fights, any disagreements, we were still fucking on the regular. "Where is this coming from?" I wanted to stand in front of him, shake his shoulders, wrap my arms around him, kiss his lips, and remind him that we were perfect for each other. But my feet wouldn't move. My breath quickened as I waited for him to respond, instead of his body, my arms wrapped around my torso, the silk of my dress not making me feel comforted.

"Destiny, I don't want to fight," he said plainly. "These past few months have shown me that we didn't have what I thought we had." My mouth opened to speak, but the words he said weren't registering. I had no response for him. I stood aside and looked down at his suitcases. "I'll call you next week to figure out the rest." His hand was on the doorknob. "I'll leave the key." It was already removed from his keyring. He placed it on the shelf near the door—the one he hung when we first moved in together, into the two-bedroom apartment we shared.

He walked out, and I locked the door behind him. I stood there until my body felt numb, and I slid down the door until I was sitting there in the pile of my dress. The tears I expected to stream down my face never came. My head slouched against the door, and I stayed in that same spot until I heard my phone alarm the next morning.

I would have been waking, beside Jensen, preparing to attend church together. Although I could have used some encouragement, a word to remind me that everything would work out despite feeling like my world was turned upside down, I was not prepared to run into Jensen.

My eyes were heavy, my head was pounding, and all I wanted to do was lay down and sleep. But as soon as I walked into the bedroom, our bed was the last place I wanted to lay. I grabbed a blanket from the closet and made myself as comfortable as possible on the couch.

Marrying Jensen was the one constant thing on my mind for at least the past few months—figuring out what was next for me, alone, was something I'd eventually have to do.

Chapter Three

Nico

As we exited the elevator, I noticed someone I hadn't seen in over two years. Although George had accompanied me from the newsroom to the lobby of the SportsOne building, my neck was straining to look at her.

He had been bragging about his alma mater being a prospective team to make it into March Madness. "If they make it, I'm placing everything on them."

Half-listening, I asked, "That confident?"

In the two years since I had last seen Destiny, it was only as she rushed through the building's lobby or behind the elevator's closing doors. Not that day, though, she was walking carefully toward the front door. I left George near the elevator, and heard him yelling, "Yo man, where are you going?" as I hurried away.

"Destiny," I shouted before she walked out. SportsOne was the place where Destiny and I first met. It may have been in the lobby then too. When I saw her back then, I invited her out for a drink, we talked for hours and went our separate ways at the end of the night. Occasionally, she'd meet at my house and watch the game with me, or we'd go out for drinks.

That was until she got in a serious relationship—she didn't directly tell me that was the reason, but I saw her out a few times with the same dude and put two and two together.

Of all the times we spent together, and even when I saw her out with him, or randomly in the building, she would have the warmest smile on her face.

It was missing, though, and when I asked, "How are you doing?" her eyes connected with mine before she quickly looked away. Then I reminded her, "It's been a really long time since we last spoke."

Without looking at me, she stated, "It has." She didn't tell me how she was doing though. I noticed her hand was rubbing the strap of her purse, incessantly, but I didn't pry.

"Plans for the night?" I asked, expecting her to tell me she had plans with her boyfriend. The man who abruptly ended our friendship.

"No." Her eyes finally met mine, and I was reminded how much I missed hanging with her. Her eyes, a shade lighter than the brown of mine, were welcoming, inviting even.

I told her, "I was headed over to grab a drink." I stared at her before asking, "Join me?"

Then the smile, it returned, and all I could do was stare at her. She had changed over the two years, gained a little weight, cut her hair—but I was easily more attracted to her now than I was a few years ago. A night out drinking may not end the same way it did back then. If she was single, and up for it, I would have shown her what we could have had together all those years ago. But I'm sure she would remind me that she wasn't looking for a quick fuck. The main reason that first night ended the way it did.

She wanted more then, and I didn't. If she wanted more now, I still didn't.

I watched her mouth form the word, "Sure," and I cocked my head, immediately thinking I was tripping.

"Really?" She nodded her head.

"Why not?" she insisted, "It's been a helluva week. And if I go home, I'll be drinking alone."

"Alone?" I repeated, not expecting her to respond. I quickly followed it up with, "Our usual place then?"

We agreed to meet at the lounge nearby, and on my bike it took me no time to get there. I arrived and found a table away from the crowd. A few minutes later she walked into the lounge and found me in the back. "Not sitting at the bar tonight?" she asked with a faint smile.

Shaking my head, I told her, "No, thought it would be nice to catch up and not have to shout over all the people over there." I nodded my head toward the bar that was crowded with people. "Do you still drink rum and Coke?"

She added, "With a twist of lime." Her hands were interlaced on the table and I noticed her ring finger was still bare. It seemed as though that was her goal a couple of years ago, to find a man, get married, and chill the fuck out. Everything counter to what I was trying to do.

"What have you been up to?" Then I teased, "Since you ghosted me?"

Her nose crinkled, then she swept her hair behind her ear. "I wouldn't call it ghosting, exactly."

"No?" I frowned.

"I mean, we weren't *dating*. Right?" I hunched my shoulders and explained she disappeared the same, and since we weren't dating there really was no need for it.

"Right." She nodded her head then looked off to the side of

us. "Sorry about that. My ugh," she hesitated, "*ex* had all my attention."

I was leaning forward because I didn't want to miss a word of the explanation. "You're single now?"

"Yes." The word lingered without further clarification. The smile on her face faded, and I considered it being a touchy topic.

Slowly, I mouthed, "Got it." Then I reassured her, "If you need to talk about it, let me know." Her laughter, loud and continuous, caught me off guard. "What?"

"It's just that," her eyes narrowed as her laughter calmed. "We didn't use to spend a lot of time talking about personal topics." Her head leaned to the side. "If it wasn't about sports, it wasn't really discussed."

I wagged my head. "I can talk about more than just sports." She looked at me, her eyes narrowed, her arms across her chest. "Honestly." Then I told her, "Try me."

"Okay, so the guy I was with, Jensen." I could only assume that was the guy I saw her with. "We were together for two years." I nodded my head. "He broke up with me Saturday." She explained how it was completely random and unexpected.

"Damn. Sorry to hear that." I wanted to tell her that's why my method was working better—no feelings, no sadness. But I could see she was hurting. "You know what?" Her brows furrowed as I said, "Fuck that dude. If he didn't want to be with you, he must be fucking crazy."

She laughed, and as she did, I wanted to keep her laughing, keep her smiling. "You've always been crazy, Nico," she whispered after taking a sip of her drink.

I informed her, "Tonight, that man doesn't even exist. Now drink up." I nodded toward her. The server was walking by, and I ordered a round of shots, despite Destiny telling me she shouldn't drink too much. "Don't worry, I'll call you a ride."

"And what about you?" I hunched my shoulders and told her I'd call one for me too. "You don't have a woman to get home to?"

I scoffed and pointed to my chest. "Me?" I leaned forward again. "Nico Maxwell? A woman at home waiting on *me*?" She nodded her head. "Guess we didn't talk about serious shit back then, huh?"

"Oh, I remember." She smirked. "Just thought maybe you changed." I shook my head. "Hmm, okay."

I held my shot glass in the air and told her, "To the single life."

She clanked her glass with mine and threw it back. After a couple more shots, she asked, "You're okay with staying single forever?" I nodded my head. "No family? Kids?"

I teased, "Uncle Nico sounds pretty good to me." Then I added, "Spoil them and send them home. If Nova has a boy, I'll have him on the court."

She winced. "And you," her words stilled for a minute before she continued, "wouldn't want a son of your own?"

The thought occurred to me over the years. Having a son who followed in my footsteps—who dominated on the basketball court. But then I thought about my disease, the fainting, the recovery, the annual check-ups. I confidently told her, "No, I think I'm good on all of that." I waved my hand in the air then asked her, "One more drink?"

She waved her hand in front of her and said, "One more drink and I may be coming home with you." Her eyebrows arched and her hand shot over her mouth.

I couldn't call the server over fast enough. I blurted, "Last round of shots then you can bring the bill." My eyes connected with Destiny's, her nose scrunched up, and she slowly shook her head. "Listen, I'm trying to see if you will come through on that threat." The waitress dropped our shots and the bill, and I pulled my phone from my pocket. "This is the last one. I'll call us a ride." Then I tilted my head and asked, "But you coming home with me or will the car be making two stops?"

She quickly told me, "Two stops," then drank the shot.

In the car, despite leaving ample space between us, I wanted to pull her closer. "I'm over here worried about a man who doesn't want me anymore," I heard her mumble from the other side of the car. I looked her way, but her eyes were set on the window. "Bet he isn't, wherever the fuck he is, worried about me." Her words were passionate, as she continued, "I bet he's already out fucking somebody." She smacked her lips. "Hell, he's probably been fucking her."

I just watched as her head twisted and turned, her mouth continued spewing words. Then the car came to a slow stop in front of my apartment. I looked at her and said, "Guess I'm first up." I leaned forward to issue a warning to the driver, "Make sure she gets home safely."

"Wait," her hand reached across the seat, and she said, "I'm coming up."

I wanted to fuck her, badly. But I still managed to ask, "You sure about that?" She nodded her head as the driver asked if we could hurry it up.

"Don't worry," I yelled to him, "I'll tip you well." I grabbed her hand from the car, and we walked to my door, neither of us saying a word.

Inside, she stood in the entry and looked around. Noting, "Not much has changed with this place either."

I laughed and told her, "Did you come to check out my place, like old times, or?"

"Right to it, huh?" She wiped a hand across her neck, as her eyes traveled the length of my body.

Chapter Four

Destiny

Who wouldn't want to fuck Nico Maxwell? The man had a gorgeous face, muscles for days, and towered over me. I could have crawled his leg and rode him till I reached ecstasy. At least that's how I had felt about him before I met Jensen. Then I had to avoid him because having a man—one who was cute too—who wanted to actually have a relationship was more important than finding a way to fuck Nico.

It wasn't just his looks though. Nico had a lot going for him. He was a co-anchor on SportsOne, a highly sought figure in college sports, and had an infectious personality.

When I realized he wasn't trying to do anything but fuck around, though, I made sure I kept things neutral with us. The last thing I needed was to fuck and fall in love with someone who would just break my heart.

His voice, the way he called out my name across the lobby caused my entire body to stall. Even if I needed to keep trekking out the exit door, I couldn't. I wanted to hear what he had to say, I needed to hear what he had to say. After years of not hearing his voice—outside of his show—I was curious.

Maybe a little hurt from the breakup, and in need of some comforting too.

I told myself, no matter what he said I would be cordial, and keep my ass moving. As vulnerable as I was, I didn't need to be near Nico Maxwell.

But then he offered to take me out for a drink, and well, that seemed harmless, right? Except, when had he ever cared about how I was feeling? When we used to kick it, our conversations only revolved around sports. And sports of all kinds—if it was basketball season, we were talking college, NBA, and even high school. Football season? He had me cheering during touchdowns. We hung out, but something about us being together was very surface level.

Neither of us crossed the line to anything more.

Telling him about Jensen, and his response, that just opened up my little legs a little further. If I didn't end up going home with him, I'd likely end up masturbating to the thought of him anyway. Might as well have the real thing, right?

Wrong. I was standing in his entryway thinking of all the ways the situation would go left. I was already fucked up over Jensen, did I need to be fucked up over Nico too?

It was too late. He had unbuttoned his shirt, and I could see his chiseled chest through his tank beneath it. There was no telling my body to back down, chill out, take my ass home. No matter how much my brain was sounding an alarm. He licked his lips and like a puppet on a string, I walked toward him.

His hand went to the side of my neck, and I no longer cared if I was about to be fucked up over Nico, because I knew I was about to be thoroughly fucked by Nico. And in that moment, my body told me that was the only thing that mattered. Our lips connected, and the kiss was magnetic. Never had I ever wanted to just kiss someone all night long like I wanted to kiss him right there in the middle of his apartment.

He reached for the hem of the blouse I was wearing and gently tugged that past my torso, releasing our kiss long enough to pull it over my head. Then his hands fumbled with my pants and the button before he finally released them down to the floor in a puddle beneath us.

It was me—bra and panties. And not even the cute pair because the last thing I expected was to end the day fucking. Let alone fucking Nico.

His hand rubbed against the cotton of my panties, and he didn't hesitate when he felt the hem that was way too high on my stomach. Nor did his hand falter when it went around to the back and felt the full coverage of my ass cheeks.

A finger meticulously navigated between the hem and my skin, then he quickly had my granny panties on the floor too. He unhooked my bra, releasing my titties and eliciting a sigh from me. He broke our kiss only to lick his tongue down my neck to my nipple where he sucked on each, alternating between the left and the right.

His mouth met mine again as his hands wrapped around my waist and he hoisted me up, walking me away from the front door. In all the times I had been to his place, I had never ventured beyond the living area. His room was off limits, then, and as he stepped through the door I considered if I should stop us before we got started. Then his tongue did this thing, where it swirled around mine, and he bit my lip after. My brain was ignored again, because all of that felt too good in my mouth, I could only imagine how it would feel against my pussy.

When he laid me down on the bed, I watched him as he

finished undressing—throwing off the shirt that was already unbuttoned, then the tank that was doing a horrible job of hiding his bulging muscles, then when he unbuckled his pants my pussy thumped. *It thumped.* Because Nico shirtless could have been on the cover of *GQ*, or *Sports Illustrated*. Hell, I could have easily stared at a billboard of him all day.

His hand was on the waist of his pants when he asked, "You sure about this?" I slowly nodded my head. "Remember I don't do love, there won't be a relationship after this."

As he continued talking, I rolled my eyes. Cutting him off, I said, "Do you give this warning to all the women before you fuck them?"

He shook his head. "No, but," his pants and briefs went to the floor, "I know you."

"Hmm," I hummed, "just bring me that dick." He laughed and walked over to the bed, his dick slanging along the way.

I could have skipped the good part, and got to the other part, but when I saw his tall ass kneel beside the bed, his eyes watching me the entire time, I held my breath in anticipation. That magic tongue he was twirling in my mouth, he twirled on my clit, and I had to remind myself to enjoy every minute of it. Because that would be it. After that night, Nico and I would go back to just being casual acquaintances.

He licked between the folds and didn't stop there. His fingers —one at a time, until I felt stretched—were inside me as he licked my clit. And I closed my eyes, enjoying every single lick and pump of his hand inside me. My mind was fogging, but through the haze I heard him say, "You ready?"

I thought I was ready. I was not. His fingers went deeper as his mouth closed around my clit; the sucking and tension combined had my legs stretching around him. The moans that escaped hid the words I wanted to whisper, "I'm not ready," and he continued until the moans became animalistic—even I didn't recognize what was coming from the pit of my belly to my mouth.

"Yeah," he said as he removed his hand and kissed the inside of my thigh. My eyes flung open as soon as I felt his presence leave from between my legs, then I was reminded of what was to come. He ripped open the condom, and with a leg propped up on the bed, he rolled it on. "Come here," he said to me as he reached out his hand.

I took his hand and let him guide me right where he wanted me, bent over in front of him. His hands were on my waist as he backed me into him, and went into me, slowly at first. I felt him bend over my back, and kiss my neck, then nibble on my earlobe.

But that was the last sweet thing he did. Everything else could have been considered nasty—in the best way. The way his fingers gripped my hair as he slapped my ass. The grunts and growls each time he flung himself deeper inside of me. Right up until I felt his hand wrap around my throat, as he thrusted one final time. Then he released me to his bed before he disappeared again.

My clothes were outside of the room, my car was parked at the bar, and I had no decent way to escape his apartment. I froze when he returned to the room, not knowing whether to curl up under the covers and let sleep take me away, or scramble to find my clothes and a ride. Then he spoke, his voice low when he said, "Alright, spending the night is not really my thing." Then he added, "I don't do cuddling after fucking," he flipped on the lamp before he added, "but feel free to make yourself comfortable in the guest bedroom till morning."

"I," my words stuttered, "ugh, sure. Okay." I stood as he made himself comfortable in his bed. I straightened my back, held my head up high, and strolled past the front of his bed without making eye contact with him. When I finally surpassed his bedroom door, I quickly gathered my scattered clothes and fumbled my way, in the dark, to the guest bedroom. My hand patted the wall until I found the light switch. Once it was flicked on, I saw the guest bedroom was nicely decorated, bed looked comfortable enough. Before jumping under the cover, though, I made my way to the bathroom and cleaned myself up.

The next morning, I woke as the sunlight just started cracking through the window. I prayed Nico wasn't a morning person as I stood from the bed, dressed, and tiptoed out of the guest bedroom to the front door. Before I could crack the door open, I heard, "Sneaking out?" with a fit of deep laughter.

My eyes clenched closed as I turned around. "Didn't see you there," I said as I opened my eyes and saw his feet were propped up on his coffee table. "Do you usually wake this early?" I asked.

He wagged his head. "Not usually, but I'm a light sleeper." He stood and walked toward me. "Maybe we can share a ride. I need to get my bike," he reminded me.

I'd been with Jensen for a couple of years, and before that I had been single for years. Occasional dates here and there, a one-night stand once or twice. But with Nico, there was something about the entire situation that was making me nervous.

"You okay?" He was standing in front of me, his eyes on me as his coffee cup went to his mouth. I fumbled with my purse, then my gaze dropped to the ground. "Wait." He picked my chin up and stared at me. "Am I making you nervous?"

I laughed. "I'm not sure what this is, but yeah, let's get out of here." I quickly turned to the door and waited for him to open it and lead the way to the ground floor where we waited on a ride.

"What do you have planned for the day?" he asked, as if everything that had transpired the night before hadn't happened.

I responded just as simply, "Some errands, a little shopping." There was a car pulling in front of us and I sighed a breath of relief. My body was tingling, even my mind was starting to betray me. The thought of one more night with Nico was circulating my mind as we climbed into the backseat.

"No invite?" I was looking out the window when he said it, and I had to ask him to repeat himself. "You aren't going to ask if I want to join you?"

My eyes narrowed as I looked his way. "What?" Then I whispered, "Was it, 'no fucking and falling in love'?"

He looked to the driver then leaned in closer to me, whispering, "I can fuck, then hang, and not once think anything about love," into my ear. "But if you can't I get it." He winked at me as he sat back against the seat.

The driver pulled to the curb in front of the bar. Nico waited for me after he stepped out. "Guess that's a no," he said as we stood there.

I bit my lip then told him, "Bye Nico," as I turned and walked away.

Chapter Five

Nico

At six foot two, one hundred seventy-five pounds, Stevie Wagner was an impressive point guard. Meeting him in his high school, on the court, before one of the biggest announcements of his career felt as exhilarating for me as it likely did for him.

It was the day I dreamed of for the first three years of my high school career, the day I'd announce which college I'd be taking my talents to.

For me, that day never came. I didn't get to stand in front of a crowd of people, with a variety of jerseys displayed in front of me. I didn't get the chance to pick it up, throw it over my head, and stand proudly with my parents cheering behind me.

As a sports journalist, I could have asked Stevie about his stats, about his impressive high school career, or how he started bouncing a ball before he spoke his first words.

My segment, *All Around*, at SportsOne was more than the sports though. I was determined to host a show that highlighted the person and not their athleticism. As I stood on the side of the court, watching Stevie bounce the ball naturally, I asked, "Outside of the court, what are you doing? What do you enjoy?"

The ball stopped bouncing, Stevie pulled the ball to his side and focused his eyes on me. "Mr. Maxwell, you played ball, right?" I nodded my head. "Did you have time for anything else off the court?" He smirked.

My dad had installed a basketball court in the driveway, and each day started with at least fifty shots before I even ate breakfast. Each night ended with at least fifty more after we finished dinner. If I wasn't traveling for the school on the weekend, I was playing in the city's league, or I was at the park near the house playing with my teammates.

If the television was on, it was tuned into SportsOne, or the local coverage of our games. I was either yelling at a competing team or cheering for a team I hoped to play for in the future. I lived and breathed basketball, and everyone in my family knew it.

It wasn't until I was discharged from the hospital after fainting that I found new hobbies. I wasn't cleared to play with my teams, or outside in the driveway; if I was at the park I could only sit on the sidelines. Watching on television irritated me for months after. I had to find a new love—my brother convinced me to learn how to play chess. It was his thing, and I was determined to have a competitive outlet; beating him was exactly the motivation I needed to learn the game.

"You know, Stevie," I finally said, "I didn't have time for anything else. It's likely one of my biggest regrets." His head cocked to the side. "That ball," I pointed to it still clutched at his side, "the court," I waved my hand through the air, "your teammates." His eyes narrowed. "Remember there's more to life than the game." Then I smiled. "You'll be great in college, maybe even make it to the NBA." I warned, "But when that's all said and done, you'll need more than the game to keep you."

He nodded his head. "Hmm..." He threw the ball up into the air, sinking it into the goal. "I can respect that."

"Good," I repeated, "Good. When you leave for college, who will you miss the most?"

His face twisted up, and I knew he wasn't used to those types of questions. But he eventually answered, "My little sister," with a smile. "She doesn't care how good I am on the court, how many points I score in a game, what teams are out here trying to recruit me." He continued, "All she cares about is if I'll read her a book or grab her favorite snack when our mom isn't looking."

"Now that," I grinned, "that is special." I adjusted my stance and took a shot at getting an *All Around* exclusive, "I know you are announcing your school tomorrow but if you'd like to throw me a bone, I'll take it." I asked him confidently, "What college will be getting your super talent?"

He jumped from his spot, soaring into the air, and touched the backboard before he laughed. "Nice try, Mr. Maxwell."

I joined Stevie and his family later that evening to conclude our exclusive with him before the big announcement. The segment we were recording would be shown before he grabbed his jersey of choice.

His little sister, Jessica, really did not care that her house was full of cameras, and that we were there to talk about her brother's amazing basketball career. She wanted to know how long it would be before she could have the fruit snacks her mom promised if she behaved. "Is it over yet?" she asked as we started walking toward the front door.

I looked over to her and announced, "It's over." Then I looked to Stevie and his parents and told them, "We'll see you tomorrow." I took one final glance around the house, trying to notice any college paraphernalia, any decorations, or coordinated colors I could glean information from. I couldn't.

On my drive to the hotel, I called my brother, the man Jessica reminded me of. Because, much like her, my basketball career didn't impress him much. When he answered, I asked, "You busy?"

Nova was always busy—even if it was the middle of the night and he was home, he often brought his work with him.

Unlike me, Nova wasn't the athlete. He was the brains of the family—instead of playing video games, he was trying to figure out how to code one. He had a dream of going to college and joining a gaming company. The day I fainted it wasn't just my basketball career that ended. It was his dream to code games. He immediately dug into data, and research, and the medical field. He was determined to find a software that could help save people from the news I received that day.

"You know me, man," Nova said into the phone. "I'm wrapping up a few things, but Harmony has told me I have another hour before I better give her some time." He laughed and I could hear Harmony in the background agreeing.

"I won't keep you too long, don't want to disrupt your time." No matter how often I tried to convince Nova to loosen up, the only one who changed him was Harmony. "And I also don't want to piss off Harmony," I laughed. She was a firecracker and I wanted to stay on her good side.

"Where are you?" Nova asked. I explained I was in Florida, with the number one recruit. "Damn, bruh, that's nice. Where's he going?" Over the years, as I started watching basketball again, Nova would watch with me. I often told him about the kids coming out of high school—top of their game.

"He wouldn't let it slip." I told him, "He's announcing in the morning though. Good kid, good family."

"I'll make sure to catch *All Around* so I can see the segment," he promised. "I didn't think you'd like being on the sidelines, but," he paused, "you actually sound happy right now."

I laughed. "I didn't think so either, Nova."

"And now that you seem to accept it, you are an okay journalist."

I interrupted him, "Okay? Man, I've never been just okay at shit." I reminded him, "Remember how quickly I picked up chess and beat your ass." He laughed.

"Cocky for damn sure," he snickered. "Anyway, Harmony has been asking if you are ready to meet one of her friends."

"I'm ready any day. You know I can meet all her single friends. There's seven days in the week." I joked, "Tell her to line them up."

Then I heard Harmony, like she was in the speaker and not off in the distance, "Nope, not at all. If you want to keep fucking around, I'm not introducing you to none of them."

"Why is Harmony so damn feisty?" was all I could say in response.

But I wasn't talking to Nova, obviously, because I could still hear Harmony loud and clear when she told me, "Because I think you are hiding your true emotions. Only fucking around so you don't have to feel something for someone. What are you afraid of, Nico?" In the few years that Harmony had been in Nova's life, she had gone from the kind girlfriend who was just around every now and again, to the very vocal wife who acted more like my sister than sister-in-law.

"Critical much, Harmony?"

"Just keeping it real, Nico. Just keeping it real," she said before telling me, "Anyway, here's your brother." Then she threatened, "Don't keep him long or I'll join him in a couple of weeks when March Madness starts."

"Shit, Harmony," I said as Nova took the phone back. I whispered, "And you think I want what you got? Fuck that." I laughed before telling him, "Man, get off the phone and make sure Harmony is nowhere near my place during the games." I knew she would be asking a million questions or asking when we could change the channel. "Don't forget to watch tomorrow."

College signing day was everything I had imagined. A crowd of people, students and administrators standing around waiting for Stevie to make his big announcement—his parents and sister standing proudly behind him. Then his coach beside them.

The *All Around* crew had our cameras rolling, waiting for Stevie to make his announcement. It was predicted that Stevie would have gone to LSU, or North Carolina, Clemson even. There were several schools offering him a scholarship so when he announced, "Next year, I'll be excited to join the Florida Gators," grabbing the orange and blue jersey to throw to his little sister, a number of people gasped in the crowd.

His eyes connected with mine, though, and I knew why he was sticking close to home.

My flight wasn't scheduled to leave until later that night, and before it did, I had an urge to fill another need. A quick trip to the hotel, and I was changed into a pair of trunks and a t-shirt I grabbed from the store next door. A short ride to the beach, then I was on the back of a jet ski speeding across the Atlantic Ocean.

The speed, the open ocean, the sun beaming down on me, was all I needed outside of the view of the women alongside the beach in their itty, bitty bikinis. Well, not all I needed, but it was the next best thing to finding a woman to fuck before my flight.

Chapter Six

Destiny

As soon as the beat dropped for "Forever My Lady" I should have just told Alexa to skip that shit, but I let it continue and by the time I heard, "Lady believe in me," I had sat on the couch and opened the photos on my phone. It wasn't the selfies, or the photos from Monroe's wedding that caught my eye, not even the bachelorette party where we had a night full of foolery. My ass had skipped to the photos of me and Jensen—six months into our relationship. Photos of our weekend trips, and him randomly around the house.

    I should have deleted the photos. I still could have. But as Jodeci continued singing in the background, I let myself scroll through them. The song was one Jensen would sing as he was in the kitchen, half-naked, making me breakfast. I would joke with him that he knew nothing about the early ninety's jams, that both of us were fresh in the crib when the songs came out. And he would say, "And how do you think either of us were made?"

The thought made my mouth grow into a slight smile. I continued scrolling, and each picture was of us cozied up, face to face, or posing in front of a city's notable landmark. We had our good times. Hell, most of the time with Jensen was beyond good, so much so that I had no doubt in my mind that we wouldn't be together forever. And as Jodeci sang, "Tell me where would I go," I considered what life without Jensen would be like.

Our breakup was awful, spontaneous, and caught me completely off guard. Okay, maybe it didn't catch me completely off guard because we were starting to have a few disagreements here and there, but I thought we were just hitting a rough patch and it would fade. I scrolled to the most recent pictures of Jensen and I together, and looking closely, nothing had changed. We were still laughing, smiling, cuddling extra close in each of those too.

As the song came to an end, I needed to know more about our breakup. What happened? I thought he owed me as much—more than he just didn't think we were working out. Before my nerves got the best of me, and the courage I had dissipated, I clicked his name and let the phone ring. And it rang, and rang, until finally he answered.

Jensen didn't go out often, and although it was a Friday night, I assumed he was at home—or wherever he was laying his head since he moved out. "Hey," I said softly as I listened for his voice.

"Destiny," the sound of my name, from his mouth, was enough to make my heart swell. The two weeks since I'd seen him, I'd thought of him every day, and almost every night. The only exception was the night I spent with Nico, but I quickly let that thought fade. "What's up?"

"'Forever My Lady' just came on," I told him. I could hear him laugh, slightly. "I was over here looking at pictures of us.

And..." then I hesitated because what? What did I want to know? My stomach started to churn, reminding me that the food I had started cooking in the kitchen was never finished.

"And what, Destiny?" he asked, his tone agitated. I wasn't used to that Jensen. I was used to the one who was my everything, all the time. The one who was concerned about how I felt and would turn the world upside down to ensure all was well with me.

"I wanted to know what happened." The words fell out of my mouth, and I continued. "I thought you were happy. I thought we were good." The more questions I had the angrier I became. "How the hell did you just end us?"

He sighed. "Destiny." I was listening. I wanted to know what he had to say. "I lose myself when we are together."

"What?" I asked, trying to recall the minutes, hours, days that made up our two-year relationship. "You lose yourself?"

"As much as I rooted for you and your career, and made sure that you were always good, I forgot about my own dreams, my own passions, what would make me happy."

"But Jensen," I argued, "you never told me any of that." I knew that he was passionate about—then I paused, because what was Jensen passionate about? He was a bank manager, and I thought his goal was to make regional director, but then I realized he never actually told me that. "Jensen, why?" I finally asked, wondering why he never shared anything with me. "You kept all this close to the chest. Even what you are truly passionate about. But why?"

"Exactly," he told me. "I never opened up to you. Despite being madly in love with you."

"And that's," I whispered, "my fault?"

He chuckled and my face grew into a scowl. I was up from the couch, trekking to the kitchen to grab a bottle of wine—

likely a bad idea considering my stomach was on empty. But I did it anyway, skipping a glass and drinking straight from the bottle. "If I tell you, it wasn't you, it was me, it'd sound like a line I was throwing." Then he told me, "But that's just it."

"And despite how much you claim to love me, instead of working on opening up, you walk away?" His words were coming to me as I chugged the bottle of wine.

"Destiny, you deserve to be happy. You deserve what Monroe has. Someone who will complete you, and not dim your light."

I was confused because I felt like my light was shining pretty fucking bright with Jensen. "My light?" I repeated. "None of this is making any sense to me." It could have had more to do with the wine I was guzzling and less to do with the words coming from his mouth, but even as I tried to concentrate on what he was saying, it sounded less and less understandable.

"Maybe it won't make sense today," he finally admitted. "But it is what it is." Then, as if he was done trying to explain, he went on to ask, "If you are home now, could I come grab the rest of my stuff?" I looked to the bedroom where I knew the closet still held more of his clothes, some of his shoes, and I agreed. "Thanks, I'll be there in about thirty minutes."

I looked down at my clothes, the oversized hoodie, the yoga pants. My hair was wrapped in a bonnet. Nothing he wouldn't have seen on a regular ass day, but if there was any chance I had left to plead my case—to make him remember what he had here at *home*—I needed to make myself a little more presentable. I placed the bottle, a quarter of wine left, in the refrigerator and ran to my room to find something to slide on. I ran the hot water in the shower and hopped in quickly to freshen up. When I was out, I checked the mirror and decided on a little makeup, but not too much, because I didn't want to be too obvious. I flung the bonnet under the sink and brushed my hair down around my face.

Two squirts of perfume to my chest and then I heard the knock at the door. My head was held high as I took each step, carefully, to let him inside. "Jensen," I acknowledged him before he walked through the door. Unlike the effort I put in to see him, he looked like he had rolled straight off the couch. His grey sweatpants—which I couldn't be mad about—and a regular ass t-shirt weren't exactly giving me *I wanted to impress you.*

"Hey, Destiny." He stood between the living room and the bedroom. "Mind if I grab my stuff?" I nodded my head and as he walked toward the closet I followed behind him. Standing close enough to watch him gather his stuff, but too far to touch him.

"Jensen, where are you staying?" I asked as he pulled clothes from the rack. He looked around, beneath the clothes, then he walked past me.

"I just need to grab a few trash bags," he huffed, "I guess." The thought of him taking his button-down shirts and Jordan's out in trash bags didn't sit well with me.

"Wait," I told him. I went into the hall closet and pulled out my luggage, the largest bags, and rolled them out. "You can return these when you're done."

He looked down at them and placed his hands on the handle. I didn't move my hand, and they touched. I looked up, hoping he felt the warmth between us. He moved his hand, touched the back of his neck, and whispered, "Thanks. I won't keep them long."

I joked, "Not like I have any trips planned, just get them back when you can." I moved my hand so he could wheel the bags toward the bedroom closet.

The luggage laid open on the floor as he stuffed in the remaining shirts, a few pants, and a jacket. I watched from the bed, sitting on the edge, trying to maintain my composure. Showing up after he had bags packed was tough, watching him pack those bags, even harder. As much as I didn't want to watch him walk out, I wanted to be near him. If I was one of my girlfriends, I'd tell her, "Girl, let that dude go. God's got someone better for you."

I knew what I would say, but I couldn't listen to myself. Something about a bird in hand, or whatever it was folks said about opportunities. The man I thought was the one for me, was right there, within an arm's reach.

He shoved his Jordan's into another bag. "I think that's just about it." I patted the bed beside me and hoped he would take me up on having a seat. "I should probably get going."

"Jensen." My voice was faint.

He had a seat beside me, and I turned to look at him. "Two years, and I just knew we were going to be together forever." I laughed. "Maybe I was naive." I looked at him, his eyes were staring at his hands folded on his lap. His shoulders were slumped. "Marriage, a bomb ass honeymoon," I continued as he sat quietly. "I even imagined what our kids would look like." My breathing was calm and I was letting myself accept that it was over. "Jensen, I want you to be happy. Whatever that looks like for you." Then my hand went over his. "Even if that isn't me. I want you to reach all your goals, pursue your passions, find a woman who you can open up to, who you can be yourself with."

His fingers interlaced with mine. "Destiny." His hand went to the side of my face. But there weren't any other words that left his mouth. He leaned in closer, his nose against mine, before our lips connected. The kiss was slow, passionate, deliberate, then he punctuated it with his hands moving down my body.

I didn't want him to stop. I wrapped my arms around his neck and pulled him down on top of me as we fell against the pillows. Our clothes were the only thing keeping us from engaging further, and he worked quickly, pulling the hem of my dress, maneuvering it up my body. I balanced on my elbows, my hips hoisted in the air, as he pulled the dress up over my head. I skipped the panties and the bra when I pulled the dress on, and he took note of my bare body as his hands glided from my chest down to the crest between my thighs.

His finger slid against the slickness, but I didn't let the pleasure of the touch slow my hands from peeling him out of his sweats, his shirt, then his boxers. He tried moving from the bed, but without any words, I gripped his ass keeping him in place.

"Please," I whispered as his dick dangled in front of my entrance.

"We shouldn't," he mumbled in response, but he only slightly hesitated.

I repeated, "Please," as my grip tightened. His lips came crashing down to mine as he entered me, and I let my body relax and take all of him in. Every inch as he took his time sliding inside. My legs wrapped around his waist, my hands went to his back, and I didn't want my body to feel what it was feeling because that meant that I was about to cum. The pleasure I was feeling would soon be over.

He slid out, but not all of him, before he slid in again. His lips moved from mine, and down to my neck, then he flipped to his side of the bed, bringing me on top of him. My eyes were closed until I felt his hand go to my face again, and our eyes connected, but he was the first to break the stare. It was a figure eight, then small circles, my hips were grinding. I lifted up, then down, but stopped as my thighs clutched around him. His hips thrust up, meeting me where I couldn't continue. Then he stopped. I rested my head on his shoulder and let my eyes gently close.

He started shifting beneath me, and I heard him say, "I should go." My eyes clutched closed, a little tighter. The stinging of the tears behind them making me turn my head to the left as I moved from on top of him. I didn't watch as he gathered the bags, walked out of the room, and out of the front door.

Chapter Seven

Nico

In my four years with SportsOne, most of my time was in the Atlanta studio. But the interview with Stevie in Florida fueled something that had me itching to get back on the road. I had just finished shooting *All Around* and was headed out of the building for the airport when I heard a familiar voice in a crowded elevator. "The new college athletic program has been doing wonders for our social media campaigns." My eyes searched the elevator until I saw her face. She was focused on the man beside her. But as the elevator doors opened and she stepped out, I followed behind.

"Destiny," I called out to her.

She turned and her eyes widened before her mouth upturned. She mumbled something to the guy who had accompanied her in the elevator before walking my way. "This isn't your floor," she said, pointing to the sign indicating we were on the sixth floor.

I explained, "I just saw you on the elevator." Her eyes narrowed. "A guy enters the elevator, six foot five, two hundred pounds, and you don't notice him?" She laughed. "You must have been deep into that conversation."

Destiny's nose crinkled and she replied, "I guess I was. Where are you headed?"

As I pressed the elevator button I told her, "I'm actually headed out of town, doing some interviews during March Madness."

Her head nodded. "Of course, your last interview broke the internet, as the kids in my department like to say. Guess they'll keep you on the road for a while?"

I popped my collar and told her, "Gotta give the people what they want." The elevator doors opened and although I needed to walk away, something about the way she looked at me wanted me to stay. I told her, "I'll catch you around." Then I stepped on, the elevators closing as she stood on the other side, her lip between her teeth.

Playing in March Madness was another childhood dream I had. Being in the arena, fans packed to capacity cheering for us, hoping we could advance in the bracket held as much weight as snagging a Division One college, or eventually a championship ring in the NBA.

I accepted that standing courtside, waiting to hit the locker room to talk to the hottest player in the NCAA, was as good as it could get outside of playing. I was there cheering and hollering as the men ran up and down the court, solidifying their chances to play at the next level with each basket they scored.

My breath hitched as the game clock ticked down, and the scoreboard inched closer to a tied game. I looked at my cameraman and told him, "I can't believe this shit." The crowd was going wild, each side cheering louder and louder. The music was blaring as the ball continued bouncing up and down the court. The ball went soaring through the air, and as it bounced off the rim, and into the hands of the man I was there to interview, I screamed, "Gahtdamn."

I slapped the cameraman's back and told him, "Let's go." He told me the game wasn't over but I looked over my shoulder, confident in David McBride's ability, and shouted, "Oh, it's over." As I heard the crowd go wild behind us, I just knew his team had won.

In the locker room, the men were going wild. I only had a few minutes between their celebrations and the time the team had to clear the locker room, so I made my way to David. We slapped hands as I congratulated him, "You've been showing out this season." He smiled wide. "What's making you play so hard?" His eyes narrowed, then he opened his locker and pointed. "Who is that?" I asked.

The picture was old, faded, and the man standing near the car was hardly recognizable. "My grandfather," he said proudly. "He didn't get to see me to this day." David looked up. "But I promised I would make him proud."

I nodded my head. "I'm sure you are doing just that. You're out here making us all proud."

"That means a lot, Mr. Maxwell, thank you." It always got me when the athletes I talked to referred to me as mister. Especially since most of them were only years younger than me, or at least it felt that way.

"Keep doing what you are doing," I told him, "On and off the court." David's stats on the court were noteworthy, and he was just as determined in the classroom. Much more determined than I had ever been in school. At least while I was playing ball. When I had to give that up, I had to put in more work in the classroom than I ever had on the court.

"You sticking around?" David asked after the cameraman pulled the camera down.

"Yeah, I'm here all week," I told him.

"When we take this thing..." He looked around at his teammates. "Make sure you are front and center to catch that interview."

"Wouldn't miss that opportunity for the world," I promised. The energy in the locker room was palpable. I walked out feeling like I had just advanced to the next seed in the bracket myself. I looked to my cameraman and asked, "Feel like going to celebrate?"

He was a little older, and we had never hung out before, but he eagerly responded, "Hell yeah."

"Alright, we'll drop this at the hotel then hit a happy hour." I offered, "I'll find a place." I had never been in Dayton, but with all the people in town for the games, I was certain someplace had to be rocking.

And it was. I found a spot not too far from the hotel for us to walk to. Jermaine had changed his outfit and looked kinda fresh. "Okay, I see you out here, Jermaine." I laughed as he slapped my hand. "Ready?"

"I may have a couple of years on you, but I'm going to show you how it's done. You can be *my* wingman for the night." He laughed.

"Oh." My eyes widened. "That's what we are on tonight?" He nodded his head. I was all game to learn from Jermaine, maybe he had a few lessons to teach me.

Inside the bar, there was a mix of college students who we actively stayed away from. Then there were some older guys watching the next games, and a few women standing around trying to look interested. We approached the bar first and ordered a couple of drinks. Jermaine told me that it was his first time covering March Madness and I replied, "Mine too. Hope after our coverage it won't be the last."

We clanked our glasses together and repeated, "To March Madness." Then his eyes started scanning the bar, and he offered, "Over there," with a slight nod of his head. He took another sip of his drink before he walked over to the ladies seated at a nearby table. "Hey ladies," he said, his voice sounding a little deeper than it was typically. "Can we join you?"

"Sure," one of them responded with a deep smile. "We were just talking about you two."

My eyes widened, and I asked, "You were?" I exchanged a look at Jermaine.

"Yeah." She looked to her friend. "I just told my friend, Corrine, that you looked very familiar." It wasn't often that women recognized me from *All Around*, or from any SportsOne programming. My show had a following, but it wasn't high in ratings for women.

Jermaine interjected before I could confirm where she could have seen me. "Yeah, my man right here has been covering March Madness in front of the camera," then he leaned in a little and said, "I've been working my magic behind the scenes."

The women nodded their heads, but the one who was speaking first shook her head. "No," with her nose crinkled, she told me, "That's not it." She went on to tell me, "It was from years ago. Did you play ball?" Then as if she remembered exactly how she knew me, she gasped. "That's it. You were that recruit in high school who collapsed, right?" Then she went on to explain that her dad was a huge basketball fan and had talked about me for months after the incident.

I wiped a hand across my chin and told her, "Unfortunately, that would be me." We continued talking, and I learned her name was Brandy. "Are you from Dayton?" I asked her as we continued talking.

"No." She shook her head. "I'm from Chicago." I nodded my head. Having been to Chicago a few times, I knew a few references.

"One of my favorite cities to eat in." I laughed. "How long are you here in Dayton?"

"I'll be here through the week." She looked to her friend, who was quite smitten with Jermaine, and said, "We thought it may be a good place to meet guys." Then she looked away from me.

"Guess you were right," I told her. I didn't ask her immediately if she wanted to join me in my room. But after talking for a couple of hours, I went ahead and threw the ball up, hoping my shot would make it when I asked, "If you don't have plans with your friend, maybe you can join me back at the hotel."

She laughed and immediately asked, "Do you find a woman in all the cities you travel in?"

I hadn't considered one of the perks of traveling for work—a new woman, one I didn't have to see ever again. The thought became real enticing. But I replied, "I just started traveling with work, I'm usually in the studio for my show, but," I didn't lie, "I'm open to the possibility." Her eyes widened and her hand flung over her mouth. I admitted, "I pride myself in honesty."

"Wow, that's brutally honest for sure." She shrugged and told me, "I wouldn't mind being the one to commit you to that decision." She took the last of her drink then leaned over to her friend and whispered in her ear.

Her friend looked at me then her, and hesitated before she warned, "Listen, I know how to find you. Anything happens to her, I'll come after you."

I threw my hands in the air and told her, "You don't have to worry about her, she's in good hands." Then I added, "At least for tonight." I winked then threw up the deuces to Jermaine.

Chapter Eight

Destiny

I had hit a slump. Sitting in my apartment was beginning to be a constant reminder of Jensen, and how no matter what, we weren't getting back together. He had cleared everything that belonged to him, so there weren't any physical reminders. I didn't have to look in the closet and see his shirts hanging or look to the floor and see his tennis shoes laying around. His shaving kit was missing from the bathroom along with the body wash and cologne that with just one whiff brought back memories of us cuddling. I stopped buying his favorite snacks at the grocery store, and the last of them were tossed out with the trash weeks after the breakup.

Even without those items reminding me of him, there was this strong tug every time I walked through the front door. If I laid on the couch and tried to watch a movie, I'd miss his presence warming me, or nudging me during the tense parts of a scary scene. If I sat at the kitchen counter, there was the loneliness I felt of eating by myself. The worst came at night, though, when it was time to turn down the covers and crawl between the cold sheets. His strong arm that would wrap around me until he fell asleep had me tossing and turning throughout the night.

I wanted to move on—I tried hanging out with my homegirls, going on a couple of dates—but nothing was helping. Weekends were the worst, especially if I didn't have plans. I was sitting on the couch, on a Friday night, watching a re-run of *Top Chef* when I had the great idea, and strong craving for whatever it was the chef was preparing on screen. A steak, with parmesan mashed potatoes, and this pea salad. My nose crinkled at the pea salad, but the steak had my mouth watering. Odd, because I didn't eat steak on the regular, and I was telling this to Monroe as I wondered the grocery store aisles. "Why didn't you just order a steak?" she was asking.

"Because," I conceded, "I need something to occupy my time. This trip around the store then cooking for a couple of hours will do just that."

She offered, "If Alex wasn't on his way home, I'd come over and help you cook, but..."

"Right, your man is on his way home, and even months after being married you two are still in the honeymoon stage." I laughed. "I get it." Although I did get it, I was feeling a little sad about her not being able to swing by and keep me company. It was like all my girlfriends were occupied with their men, or other plans, and I was alone. Usually that wasn't a problem, but for some reason it was reason enough to have me about to cry in the dairy aisle. I told Monroe, "I've been like super emotional lately."

"You have?" she asked.

I nodded my head. "Yeah. I bet Mercury is in retrograde." I went on to tell her how I learned all about moon cycles and how they fuck up your emotions. "It's really quite interesting actually." I continued walking the aisles of the store and found myself near the personal care items. I passed the soap aisle and almost considered buying Jensen's body wash, to just have it around, then I thought, *Why would I torture myself?*

I did grab the bottle, open the cap, and take a whiff. But instantly, my stomach churned. I had to laugh and tell Monroe, "How crazy is it that I just sniffed Jensen's body wash?"

"What? Okay, clearly you need an intervention," she announced. "What is going on with you?"

But then I assured her, "Don't worry, my body is on the same page because my stomach turned when I smelled it. Guess it's just my heart that can't get it together."

"Your stomach turned?" As she was talking, I walked down the aisle for feminine products and thought I should grab a pack of tampons. I paused to check for my favorite brand, when I heard Monroe mumble, "Destiny, random cravings, stomach turning when you smelled the soap, overly emotional."

And before she could say anything else, I whisper shouted, "I'll call you back," into the phone, before hanging up, not waiting for her reply. I pulled up the period app that I consistently updated to check for my last period. Before I could get very far, the app alerted me that my period was late. *Late.*

My face went flush, and I felt like the little food I had in my stomach was making its way up my throat. "Oh gosh," I said to myself as my hand went to my head. I leaned over my grocery cart and made myself breathe, slowly. "This can't be right."

Despite what the app was telling me, I made myself remember the last time I had my period. It was before Monroe's wedding. "Okay," I whispered as I flipped the calendar back a month to her wedding date. Then I flipped it through each week after her wedding and counted.

It's because I've been in my feelings, my body is off. Then I thought, *Could Mercury Retrograde fuck up my period too?* I closed my eyes and chastised myself for that dumb ass idea. My head scanned the tampons, then the pregnancy test. I bit my lip as I found one that read "Pregnant" as a result instead of the plus sign, because the last thing I needed was ambiguity. If it was happening, I needed to be sure.

I dropped the box into my cart and made my way to the front of the store. The clerk, a young woman with a bright smile, grabbed the pregnancy test from the belt and looked at me. In the softest voice, she whispered, "Good luck."

My eyes blinked, and I gave her no response. Would good luck be a positive pregnancy test? Or would good luck be a negative, and no connection to the man who broke my heart? I shoved my card into the slot and grabbed my bags, walking out of the store without noticing anything or anyone else around me.

It wasn't until I was buckled into my seat that I paused before beating my hands against the steering wheel. I yelled, "How?" before the stream of tears rolled down my face.

On the way home, I managed to be stopped by every single red light. The elevator to the lobby had to stop on each of the building's six floors before opening in front of me, then each of the four floors below me before getting to my floor.

I walked quickly to my apartment, and inside I threw my bags to the floor and made my way to the bathroom. I ripped the box open, laid it on the counter, and read through the instructions. Pee on the stick, wait five minutes, read the results. Simple enough.

Except, of all the times I needed to pee on demand, I sat on the toilet and nothing. Not even a drip. I reached over to the sink and let the water stream until I felt my bladder respond. There wasn't much, but enough to cover the dipstick. I laid out tissue on the counter, then laid the test right on top of it.

After washing my hands, I closed my eyes then re-opened them. The test had no results. I paced the floor between my bedroom and the bathroom, breathing hard as I did.

My phone was ringing in the kitchen, but I decided whoever it was could wait. I stopped pacing and looked down at the pregnancy test. It read, "Pregnant." And I blurted, "Fuck."

My hand immediately went to my stomach, then I was down on my knees, my head over the toilet as I heaved out the lunch I had digested. The box came with two tests. Probably for moments such as that. I took it out, sat on the toilet, and repeated the whole process again. This time the pee came streaming. I sat that test on the counter and waited.

Instead of pacing, I went to the kitchen, grabbed my phone, and saw the missed call was from Monroe. Before calling her back, I returned to the bathroom and peeked at the second pregnancy test. "Pregnant," it read.

Monroe answered her phone on the first ring, and I could hear her talking to Alex in the background. "What happened?" Then she asked more questions while I just sat silent. I moved to the kitchen and started unpacking the bags.

In my haste, I had only managed to purchase a box of mashed potatoes and milk. No steak. I shook my head, opened my refrigerator, and pulled out a box of Chinese leftovers. "Well," I told Monroe, "I was in the store and checked my period app."

"Okay," she said slowly, "And?"

"Said I was late."

"Did you grab a pregnancy test?" Before she could ask any other questions, I went ahead and told her both tests were positive.

"Oh shit." She was sitting silently before she offered, "Should I come over?" Then before I could respond, she told me, "Yeah, I'm coming over. I'll be right there." I heard her talking to Alex in the background before she told me, "I'll see you in a bit." The phone had hung up, but it remained at my ear. I took a deep breath because I didn't want to be alone, but I also didn't want to discuss my next steps.

I knew it had to happen. I could have only been a few weeks along, but I had to make a decision. Whatever that decision was, though, I didn't have it in me to talk about. Instead, I wanted to just sit on my couch, with my Chinese leftovers, and cry. A tear rolled down my cheek as if I cued it. When I cried watching a dating show the week prior I should have known something was up. Fuck.

I put the phone on the counter and placed the takeout container in the microwave. As it warmed, I could smell the scent of the beef and broccoli. At first it smelled like nourishment and abundance. Then it smelled like the back of a garbage truck, and suddenly my stomach felt like it was going to hurl out of my mouth.

The bathroom floor was becoming my best friend, and the coolness alone was enough to satisfy me. Knocking at my door then booming a minute later made me move from my coveted spot where I just waited for my stomach to relieve itself; it never came. I opened the front door, my shoulders sunken, my face tear-stained, and my hair likely tangled from rubbing my hands through it.

I knew I looked a complete mess, and Monroe confirmed that when her eyes widened and she whispered, "Damn," before she walked through the door. "Do you need anything?" She looked around the apartment. "How can I help?"

I appreciated her effort, but I didn't even know what I needed at the time. In honesty, I replied, "I don't know what you can do for me." My lips poked out and I sighed. "I should probably just sit down. I want to eat, but the smell of the food made me nauseous."

Her nose turned up and she offered, "Maybe you need something bland." She made her way to the kitchen and started opening and closing cabinet doors. "You have to have some crackers in here."

"Yes," I quickly replied, "Next to the refrigerator, cabinet at the top."

"Wine crackers," she laughed. "I guess that'll do."

She eased herself down on the couch beside me, her gentle movement making me ask, "What are you doing?"

"I don't know, just feel like you may be fragile right now." We both laughed. She opened the crackers and handed one to me. "Do you want to talk about it?" Her voice was soft, apprehensive.

I shook my head. "I know I need to though." She sat beside me quietly until I started to speak again. "God has a funny way of doing things, right?"

She turned to face me with her legs curled under her. She handed me another cracker and I bit then chewed on it slowly, letting it glide down my mouth carefully.

My fingers were tapping alongside my thigh when I said, "I always said I wanted kids with Jensen." I smirked. "But I never wanted to be like my mom. I didn't want to have to raise a kid on my own. That's not what I wanted."

"Oh." Monroe placed a hand to her heart, then she pulled me into her with her free hand. "Destiny, if you decide to have a baby, you won't be alone."

I pulled away, a fresh stream of tears making their way down my face. "Of course not, my mom had a slew of family and friends around, if she needed them, but..." I shook my head. "I saw her late at night, when it was just her. Early in the morning. When she had to miss work for all my events. I know how hard it was on her. Despite being supportive and telling me she was stronger for having me, I know how hard it was for her." My hand went to my face and swiped at the constant flow of tears, then it flopped into my lap carelessly. "Not to mention what it would be like bringing a baby home, alone." I scoffed. "Even my dad was around for my early years."

My dad left my mom when I was about five years old, and she had stayed single all those years, only recently starting a committed relationship. My dad came around, sparingly, but he was in no way around enough to help. Over the years I stopped wondering if she would ever re-marry, and realized she was married to her career. Becoming a successful lawyer became her one and only goal in life.

"And if you told Jensen, you think he would not want to be a part of his child's life?"

"Maybe he would," I told her, "But would I want that for the baby?" I frowned. "Or for me?"

"Okay, do you want to talk about your *other* options?" She gulped. My eyes closed as the options, the ones that all flashed in my mind earlier, came back to my thoughts. "Or, we don't have to talk about it now. Let me know how I can help."

"Can I tell you something?"

She mouthed, "Of course."

"The week after your wedding." I let that timeline sink in. "I saw Nico in the lobby of our office building." Monroe didn't budge, I knew she was all ears. "We met for drinks, then after, I went to his place and we..." I let my sentence trail off as I plucked at the hem of my shirt.

"Oh." Her eyes widened. "Oh." She was silent, then she asked, "Do you think?"

I shook my head feverishly. "Absolutely not. We used a condom. I'm certain this is Jensen's baby."

"Would you have wanted something with Nico, if it were an option?"

My shoulders hunched up to my ears. "I don't think it would ever be an option. Nothing has changed with him." Monroe knew how much I was into Nico when we used to hang out years prior. She knew that I was infatuated, lusting after a man I knew was untouchable. Because for me, I didn't want to just fuck and walk away, I wanted to fall in love.

"But you fucked him anyway?"

I cringed. "Yeah."

"Alright." She looked away from me then declared, "Well, guess nothing changes there. And nothing changes with Jensen." She reached for my hand, pulling it from the entanglement it had with the unraveled thread. "The decision is all yours to make, and no matter what you decide, I got your back."

Chapter Nine

Nico

Months on the road started with March Madness, then spiraled into *All Around* doing a road show. We visited different universities, as they recruited with the new NIL deals, and talked to recruits about their expected performance for the season. I'd traveled from Ohio, to DC, up the east coast, and down the west. But when Nova called me and told me I needed to be home for my mama's birthday, I was happy to oblige.

Besides missing my bike, I missed my bed. The hotels, in all their comforts, still weren't home. Although, having a new woman, in a new zip code, every couple of nights didn't hurt. I wasn't mad about being back in my own place though.

Seeing my mom's face light up when I walked through the door added a little more incentive. She had insisted we all meet at her favorite steak house in the city, and when I walked in, she, my dad, Nova, and Harmony were all standing waiting for the hostess to return to the stand. "Nico," my mom outstretched her arms, "I'm so happy you are home." I rubbed her back and kissed her forehead.

"I wouldn't dare miss your birthday, Mama." I exchanged a glance at Nova. It was him who called reminding me of our mom's birthday. Each year he had to do the same, urging me to be wherever she wanted us, when she wanted us there.

The hostess had returned, and our father took lead on announcing our reservations. As we waited for her to collect menus and silverware, I saw someone who looked vaguely familiar walking our way.

My parents and Harmony followed behind the hostess, but my feet wouldn't move. I narrowed my eyes and tilted my head, trying to figure out if it could really be Destiny. If it was, she was carrying much more weight on her than the last time we saw each other. And it was all centered in her belly. *"Wow."* My mouth dropped when I realized it was her, and she was pregnant.

Nova turned to me and asked, "You good?" I nodded my head and he walked behind the group to the table, but I stayed behind to speak to Destiny.

She was with a woman I had never seen before when I said her name, "Destiny," and they both stopped in front of me.

Destiny looked to the woman and nodded before she waved and continued walking out of the building. "Hey," I said softly. With my head still tilted, I asked, "How are you?"

A small smirk came up on her face and she answered, "That's a little complicated."

I let my eyes travel from hers and land on her belly before I responded, "It looks like I should be telling you congratulations though?" Her mouth didn't morph into a smile, and in fact, she frowned. Her hand was rubbing her belly though.

"Thanks," she whispered. We were standing in the middle of the restaurant lobby, and although I wanted to ask more questions, ask how she was doing, we had people passing by. "I should probably get out of here," she told me.

I reached out and wrapped an arm around her shoulders, pulling her closely into me. Then I leaned into her ear and told her, "It was good seeing you." As she pulled away and walked to the door I watched in amazement.

By the time I found my family, they were all seated around a table in a private room. An empty seat next to Nova. When I sat down the server came by and asked what I wanted to drink. I responded, "A whiskey, on the rocks," without hesitation.

Nova nudged me in the side and asked, "You good, bruh?" I was browsing the menu, my mind still on Destiny and her very pregnant belly. "What happened?" Nova asked, and I looked up from the menu.

"Remember Destiny?" I asked him. The look on his face didn't turn to one of recognition so I began detailing how he'd know her. "We used to kick it a while back, she was over a few times when you would stop by." Then I laughed. "In fact, she's the one who tried to convince you to make me spokesperson for HealthScare before your little COO knocked the idea down."

He cocked his head to the side, then he said, "Oh, right. I remember her." Then his eyes narrowed, and he asked, "Was she pregnant?"

I nodded my head. "She was." But when he asked when the last time I saw her was I ignored that and instead brought my attention back to the menu. Thankful for the server asking for our entrée orders.

My mom's gardening, my dad's impeding retirement, and Harmony's joy for everything nerdy was enough to keep us talking about everything but Destiny and her baby bump.

But the topic of babies wasn't something that was off the table. My mom was discussing future grandbabies with

Harmony when Nova looked to me and asked, "What about Nico, Ma?"

Both my dad and her looked my way. "Nico?" my mom asked. "Is that something you are ready for?"

I deflected, "Where are you two headed for vacation next week?"

"See, neither of our boys want to make us grandparents." My mom looked to my dad and feigned despair. "One year, I'm going to ask for grandbabies for my birthday, and every other holiday." Then she squealed, "A Christmas baby, how great would that be?"

Then my dad, likely tired of the conversation, announced, "And tonight, there's supposed to be a live band." He stretched his neck. "When we finish our dinner, we can have a little dance."

"Yes," I proclaimed, "dance the night away." We all laughed.

The more I considered her question, though, I thought about Destiny, and how the last time I saw her she was very single. Could she have rekindled with her ex? Or could she have quickly moved on to someone else?

On the road, her name came up often, not because I mentioned it but because she had become a marketing aficionado for *All Around*. It was her talents that doubled our audience, and likely kept me on the road. Each time someone mentioned her name, telling us the advice she had given me or my co-host to help promote the show on social media, I would think about our time together. Not just the time we fucked, but the times before that when we were just kicking it.

We could hang, watch sports, and share food—for hours at a time. She'd come over dressed down, like a pair of sweats and a baggy shirt would hide her undeniable curves or make me any less attracted to her. Eventually, though, it wasn't my sexual attraction to her that was at the forefront of my mind.

I was in a daze, staring at my empty glass while everyone around me was chatting, my dad leading the way telling stories about my mom in her younger years. "You know, I think you are as hot now as you were in your twenties." I looked up to see my mom grinning. "Now," my dad stood from his seat, "You owe me a dance." My mom stood, grabbing his hand.

They left the room smiling and laughing. Then I was left with the other couple, who couldn't get enough of each other. Harmony was leaning over Nova, whispering in his ear, and I announced, "I think I'm going to check on out." But before I left, I told Nova, "I'll take care of the check on my way out."

He shook his head, telling me, "You know I can't let you do that." Then he laughed. "Always trying to step in and play the favorite son." Usually, I'd argue, but I let him have it.

"You know what," I tapped his shoulder, "You got it." On my way out of the restaurant, I stopped by the bar and found a seat next to a gorgeous woman.

She was sitting with a friend, who was almost as gorgeous as she was. And when I ordered a drink, she leaned over and spoke before I had the chance to make my own introduction. "Drinking alone?"

"Unless the two of you would like company." I looked between both of them.

"Wouldn't mind at all." She raised her glass in the air and declared, "To new friends."

I repeated, "To new friends."

Our conversation ranged from casual to personal before I even finished my drink. The woman seated closest to me asking, "Did you approach hoping to take one of us home tonight?" I couldn't help but smile at her bold style. It wasn't usually the woman who shot her shot, at least not with me. I saw what I wanted and had no problem going after it.

There was only one way to answer her, with complete honesty. "I wouldn't mind." Then I challenged, "but not just one of you." I paused and waited for either of them to become defensive, and when they didn't, I asked, "What would you say to that?"

It was the other woman who was finally speaking up. "Can't say it'd be the first time we had the offer." Then she smiled at her homegirl and said, "Or the first time we accepted it." With her glass to her lips, she finished off her drink. Then she licked her tongue across her lips and said, "V, what do you think? Think he can handle us?" Her hand moved to *V's* lower back, and V's hand went to my forearm.

"I don't know if he can handle us," V stared me down, "but I'm willing to give him a try."

Being back in Atlanta, I could have easily brought the women to my place, but I noted, "Two against one, I feel like I should be on your territory and not mine. So maybe you two are taking me home tonight."

They didn't hesitate, asking for my phone. "I'll drop my address in your phone." I handed it over. "And we'll meet you there."

"I'll meet you there." The two of them stood from the bar and walked out. I was right behind them. Before I left, I looked over my shoulder and smiled at my parents dancing across the floor.

I pulled my bike into a parking spot near the front of their building. On my walk to the door—of whoever's apartment—I untied my tie, unbuttoned my top buttons, and by the time I was at their door I was ready for whatever was on the other side.

It was V who answered the door. "Come in." She grabbed my tie, tugging me through the door. "You look a little," her eyes glanced over my face, "uneasy." She laughed. "Is this your first threesome?"

"What?" Then I stammered, "Of course not." Then I admitted, "The two of you are," I looked over her shoulder in search of her homegirl, "where is your homegirl anyway." The two of them were catching me off guard. I had to roll my shoulders back and put my game face on.

"D, she's," she pointed toward the bedroom door, "in the room waiting for us."

"Okay," I grabbed her hand and told her, "I'll follow you."

She did just that. The door opened and D was laying across the bed, with a wine glass in her hand. "Come here," she told me as she sat her glass down on the table beside the bed. She looked at V and said, "He looks a little nervous, huh?" They both laughed. "How about you sit right here." I sat on the edge of the bed. "And you come here." She pulled V by the hem of her dress, and their mouths connected as I watched. Hands were roaming, clothes were thrown to the floor, and I had a glimpse of a titty before I decided to join the party.

I couldn't easily find where I fit in. I started with a hand on each of them until D turned to me her mouth, meeting mine. As our tongues intertwined, I felt another mouth along my neck. Their moans became synchronized as we coordinated our moves. V and me, them together, then them kissing me.

Speeding down 285 on my bike had nothing on the adrenaline rush I had sitting between the two of them while one sucked my dick, and the other hovered over my head her pussy covering my mouth.

Two women—meant two times the orgasms. My stamina didn't fail me, and I thrusted into one while my hand played with the other. It was D who tapped out first, collapsing beside us.

Her exhaustion didn't stop her from watching as I grabbed V's hips, slowly entering her over, and over, and over again.

She finished with a piercing scream before she fell to the pillow. "So?" I said as I slid between the two of them.

"Yeah," it was D confirming that, "you can come over whenever you like."

I considered the offer but didn't respond. Instead, I climbed out of the bed, and after cleaning up and dressing I told them, "This was fun. I'll let myself out." Neither asked me to stay, and I only heard mumbles as I walked to the front door.

When I left the restaurant, I could have easily taken my ass home—but for some reason, I needed an outlet for my thoughts. Thoughts that were still stuck on Destiny, and the bump she had growing. Fucking one woman would have usually done the job, fucking two definitely should have cleared my head.

Instead, I wracked my brain as I walked to my bike. Because the only thing that kept floating in my mind was the last time I fucked Destiny, and I tested my math skills trying to figure out if that time could have possibly aligned with her pregnancy.

Of course, I knew condoms weren't one-hundred-percent fool proof, but we used one. If she knew I was the father—I climbed on the back of my bike— there was no doubt she would have told me.

My helmet was strapped on my head, and the bike shifted into gear as I sped toward the highway. "Of course," I whispered to myself, "she would have told me."

Chapter Ten

Destiny

Getting around, in Atlanta, middle of the summer—with a growing belly was making me second guess leaving the house. For anything. Let alone a trip to my mom's house.

I had avoided her for the first twelve weeks, not telling her I was pregnant until I knew exactly what I wanted to do. When I decided I would keep the baby, even if that meant that I'd be a single mom like her, I shared the good news.

Since then, she was either at my apartment, or was begging me to come to her house. I didn't know whether I loved the attention or hated it. But with the heat reaching nearly one hundred degrees, I was tempted to bow out of the visit. I knew I wouldn't hear the end of it, though, so I walked, confidently, to the parking garage.

The drive through traffic took longer than necessary, and by the time I was pulling into her driveway, I was praying she had a snack, a meal, a refrigerator full of food. "Hey, Mama," I said as soon as she opened the front door.

"My babies." She grinned and held her arms open, but not at shoulder height. Her arms were headed for my stomach, her lips puckered up to kiss my protruding belly button.

"Mom," I said as she continued rambling to my stomach. "You know what your baby actually needs?" She stood and smiled. "Some food," I blurted.

"Oh," she moved away from her doorway, "of course." As I walked to the kitchen she gushed, "I don't cook with pears often, but I wanted something to recognize the baby's size," from behind me. I entered the kitchen and saw the platters lined on the counter.

"Mom," I looked over my shoulder at her, "What is all of this?"

She explained, "A pear crisp," then her hands went over a salad bowl, "A salad topped with pears." Then she pointed to a plate of muffins, "And pear muffins." My nose curled up. "None of that sound appetizing?" She quickly turned to the refrigerator. "I can cook something else." She started pulling out containers, placing them on the counter. "What are you craving?"

I put my hand up. "Mom." I sighed. "Slow your roll."

My mom had always been over the top. Despite the fact that she was likely exhausted from her job, she prepared food for the bake sales, volunteered for the field trips, and made a home-cooked meal on most nights. "Am I doing too much?"

"The most." I laughed. "I don't think I even like pears." Then I cringed. "And the thought of the baby being the size of a pear and eating pears seems a little," I hesitated, "Off putting."

Her shoulders hunched up to her ears and she put a hand to her face. "Right," she gritted her teeth, "That may seem a little cannibalistic, right?" I nodded my head.

"Okay," she peeked inside of a container, "I have smothered chicken and mashed potatoes." Then she held up another container, "and peas."

I went to the cabinet and pulled down a plate. "Now, that's what I'm talking about." Then I thought, "Wait, who did you cook all this food for anyway?" I knew that my mom had a little boyfriend, someone who had been at her house on a handful of times while I was visiting. "Was this for Taylor?"

She turned her back. "I think I even have rolls in here."

"Oh no, you had a lot to say when you were telling me all the different ways you cooked a pear."

Before she could place the plate in the microwave, I leaned over her, fork in hand, and scooped up a forkful of potatoes. "Yum," I hummed. "Get those warmed up ASAP." I found my way to a chair at the counter and rested my feet. "To think I was going to stay home today."

She gasped. "Wait? What? You were about to stay home today?"

I put a finger in the air. "No ma'am." I shook my head. "You first. Was all that food for Taylor, are the two of you getting closer?"

She leaned against the counter and admitted, "Yes, I think Taylor and I are getting pretty close." Her face grew into the most beautiful smile, and I felt the emotions from earlier in my pregnancy returning. "We are thinking," she paused and looked at me, "Destiny, are you crying?"

I covered my face and laughed, then felt her arms around my shoulders. "I thought this part was over. But I'm happy for you." My hand went to my stomach. "You deserve someone who will love you unconditionally, Mama." My heart grew fuller.

"Okay," she said with a kiss to my forehead as the microwave dinged. "Why were you going to stay home today?"

My plate was balanced on her hand, she grabbed a napkin and placed them both in front of me. Before telling her anything, I scooped a piece of chicken and mashed potatoes into my mouth. A couple of bites later, and I was ready to tell her. "It's just that it's so hot outside. I didn't want to leave the cool air, not even for a minute." She laughed and told me she half-understood. "And, it's also that you are a little more excited than I am." Her eyes widened, but she took her time with a reply.

"Destiny, you aren't that fiery high schooler anymore, you conquered college, and you are doing well for yourself now. Having a baby, and raising it alone, isn't something to be down about."

"That's just it," I argued, "I'm not down about raising this baby alone." I scooped more food into my mouth before I continued, "I don't know if I want to tell Jensen."

The ice machine refilling, the air conditioner running, the birds chirping outside were all sounds that were louder than the silence in the kitchen during that moment. The more I spoke, the less my mom could find words to say. When she finally did, I could have done without them. "Your father was around when he wanted to be. He had the leisure of dropping in when he had time. Sending gifts if he remembered."

"Mom," I interrupted, not knowing where she was going but wherever it was, I wasn't interested in hearing it. "Dad is the last person I want to even think about right now."

"He may be the last person, but I think you need to keep that in mind as you consider what you will do with," she paused, "Jensen."

I narrowed my eyes. "Wait, what was that?" My finger dangled in the air.

"Well..." She placed a hand on my thigh. "You and Jensen broke up after the wedding, right?" I nodded my head. "And without getting in your business." She cocked her head. "The math doesn't add up."

Sex wasn't something that was exactly out of the ordinary for us. The birds and the bees, where babies came from, all of that was discussed when I was in middle school. After that, our conversations centered around birth control, and that was about it. At all costs, I avoided discussing my sex life with my mother. And hers, well that was absolutely not a topic of discussion. "Stuff happens, Mom," I sighed. She nodded her head.

"Okay, so Jensen." She was definitive. "You should be okay with the fact that he may very well go on with his life. And you may never get from him what you expect."

"And," I placed my fork on the plate, "you think the answer is to not tell him I'm pregnant?"

She hunched her shoulders. "I'm not saying not tell him. I'm advising you to prepare yourself for him not being there for you when you need him." Then she told me, "But don't worry, Destiny, you can do this alone. And I'll be here for you every step of the way."

I laughed. "You know, I considered all my options." I rubbed my hand across my stomach. While she watched me, a blank stare on her face, I explained, "Abortion. It was an option, but even after making the appointment, I felt like I would never be able to go through with it." My hand tapped the counter. "Then there was adoption, and that didn't feel any better."

"Destiny, I'm glad you are going to raise your baby."

I scoffed. "You know what I fear more than anything?" She cocked her head. "Being stressed out, losing myself, or not being an adequate mom."

I felt her arms around me again as she said, "Destiny, I wish I could tell you those thoughts would never come, but the truth is, being a mother will come with doubt. Stress. Anxiety." Then she smiled. "But also hope, excitement, unconditional love.

"Thanks, Mom," I told her. "I know I can do this alone." I felt the sadness returning. "If I have to." Then I let her know, "Dad wasn't around, but I still know who he is. And I would never take that away from this baby."

She walked to the refrigerator and asked, "Would you like a water?" I nodded my head. "I'm glad you made that decision. And I hope that Jensen will be responsible." She sounded skeptical but I ignored that.

Then I told her, "He may not be who I want him to be as a father, but not telling him isn't an option. And trying to make it work." I shrugged. "It won't."

"When do you plan on telling him?" The last time I spoke to Jensen was the night he walked out with all of his shit. Not a single text, phone call, or visit happened since. And the thought of calling him to tell him that I was pregnant was daunting. When I didn't answer, she told me, "You have twenty-three weeks, or you'll be introducing him to the baby."

"Right." Twenty-three weeks had my head spinning, and telling Jensen I was pregnant before that had me feeling like I was going to throw up. My face was flush, and my hands became clammy. I just wanted to crawl into my bed, and lay, naked. So, I told my mom, "I should get going." I looked over at the pear muffin and said, "I'm going to take one of these to go." She laughed.

On the ride home I couldn't stop thinking about how I would tell Jensen. A text message, over the phone, in person. My nose crinkled. Then I thought, if he was or wasn't going to be in the baby's life, it didn't matter much while I was pregnant. I wouldn't expect him to show up to appointments, bring me anything for my cravings, or rub my aching back or feet. Whether I told him now, or waited, what would I gain?

Chapter Eleven

Nico

I had Destiny's phone number, and in the couple of weeks that had passed since I saw her in the restaurant, I considered calling her. That never happened, there were a few written and erased text messages. Several times I stared at her contact information in my phone, my finger hovering over her phone number. There were even times I thought about requesting her presence at an *All Around* meeting. She was the marketing expert, after all, and I could have come up with a question or two for her.

None of that happened, though there was something about the entire situation that wasn't sitting right with me.

When I saw her, in the SportsOne lobby, I knew I should have left well enough alone, but I approached her anyway. "Destiny," I said as she made her way across to the front door. Much slower than usual, her steps cautious. It didn't take long for my extra-long strides to catch up with her. "Hey," I said. I looked around us and asked, "Mind if I talk to you over here?"

She looked around her, then over to the spot I pointed to, and whispered, "Sure."

We were standing there across from each other, and I couldn't find the words I had been wanting to ask her over the phone since the last time I saw her. Finally, I blurted, softly, "Last time I saw you, I didn't get a chance to ask."

"Ask what?" Her smile disappeared.

"When are you due?" The extent of my pregnancy knowledge stopped with the fucking it took to get a woman pregnant. I knew a woman carried a baby for nine months, then went to the hospital and home the baby came.

She told me she was due in November, and I just nodded my head. "And how are you feeling?" I asked, not wanting to stand in front of her and count back to our little encounter.

"Hot and bothered." She laughed. "And not the way I used to like to feel hot and bothered."

With that little comment she had me missing our banter. "I bet. Do you need anything?" I wanted to extend the time we had together, not knowing the next time I would see her. "Ice cream, an Icee, a fan with a bowl of ice in front?" I asked.

She declined my offer and told me, "I was actually headed to Monroe's house." The name escaped her mouth as if I should have known it. I guess she realized that too when she added, "That's who was with me last time I saw you." Then she told me, "My birthday weekend. At the restaurant."

My mouth formed an, "Oh," then I told her, "I don't think I realized you shared a birthday with my mom." I explained, "I was there to celebrate her."

"Who knew?" She winked. "She must be an amazing woman."

"And she is." I don't know where the thoughts were coming from, but something had me wanting to tell her she was also amazing, but I stopped myself before they could escape my mouth. "I won't keep you." Before she walked away I said, "But if you are free this weekend, I'll be sure to have the ice on deck."

She reached an arm out and I leaned into her, her stomach creating a barrier between us. "I'll keep that in mind. Thank you, Nico." Then she turned and walked away.

On my way home, I called my brother and told him, "I need you to meet me at my house."

"Man, you know it's a holiday weekend, right?" Of course, I knew it was a holiday weekend, it was the only reason I was back in Atlanta again.

I didn't know what that had to do with him meeting me at my house though. "And?"

"And I'm prepping for the barbecue your ass is supposed to be at tomorrow." He huffed. "What's the problem anyway?"

My head turned to the glass window that surrounded the SportsOne building and my eyes followed Destiny as she walked. "I think I got a woman pregnant."

He didn't hesitate when he responded, "I'll be there in fifteen." I knew very well it took him at least thirty minutes to get from his office, or his house to my place, but I appreciated the urgency he was applying. Because if it was true, I needed all the advice I could shake from him.

Although he promised fifteen minutes, I was pacing my floor in front of my television as I waited for him to arrive. The television wasn't even on, and although I was in complete silence, the thoughts in my head were yelling. Nova knocked on my door, like the damn police, and I took a deep breath before I jogged over to open it.

"Pregnant?" he asked before he said anything else.

"Ugh." I walked back to my living room and continued the

trek of pacing I had before he arrived. He sat on the couch, his elbows resting on his thighs. "Okay, so Destiny."

"Destiny. Like the girl you used to kick it with?" I nodded my head. "The one you just saw a couple of weeks ago? That Destiny?" I confirmed. "And the only way you could have gotten her pregnant is, if..." He stood from the couch and his hand went to my shoulder.

"Bruh," I told him, "I know how a woman gets pregnant." I laughed. "May not know much else about pregnant women, but I know what fucking can lead to."

Then he asked, "As much as you are out here fucking, don't tell me you aren't using condoms." He slapped my shoulder.

"Hell naw, I'm always strapped up." I frowned. "And I get tested regularly. You don't have to worry about that," I assured him. "But you and I both know that condoms aren't full proof."

He gave me a sideway glance. "Yet you still out here fucking anything walking."

I hung my head. "C'mon, man."

"Okay, okay, so you think Destiny is pregnant and it's your child." He rubbed his hand across his head. "What makes you think that?" Then I explained I did the math, calculating her due date to the one and only time we fucked. "And you only slept with her once?" I nodded my head. "I don't know, man. I don't think she would be in your face and not tell you the baby is yours." He moved to the other side of the room before stating the obvious, "Why don't you just ask her?" As apparent as it was, it wasn't something I was ready to do.

"And what if it is my baby?"

He coughed. I was still pacing the floor, and when I looked up again, so was he. "Listen, one thing at a time. First thing you need to do is find out if it's your baby."

"Right," I stopped pacing and told him again, "Right." I

knew she had plans, but I didn't want to wait another night to find out if Destiny was carrying my baby. I wanted to know. "Hey man," I wrapped an arm around his neck, "thanks for this."

"You know I got you, bruh, always." I patted his head.

"I know." As he walked to the door, I grabbed my phone and looked at him. "I'll call you after I talk to her."

"Bet." He waved his hand and walked out the door.

Before I could call her, though, I went to the kitchen, grabbed a glass, filled it with a few cubes of ice, then poured Hennessey over it. "Alright," I said to myself after it went down my throat.

I held the phone in my hand, clicked on Destiny's name, then closed my eyes before I opened them again and clicked on her number. The phone was clutched to my ear, and I listened to each ring. Four before I heard them stop. I waited for her voicemail, and when I heard her voice repeating, "Hello?" I paused instead of speaking. "Nico?"

"Hey, Destiny." I started quickly telling her, "I know you had plans tonight, and I hope I'm not interrupting, but—"

Then it was her that stopped me from continuing. "Nico, yeah, I'm still at Monroe's house."

"Do you mind if I take up a few more minutes of your time?" I really didn't want to wait.

"Give me just a minute." I could hear people in the background. Then it was quiet. "Okay. What's going on?"

"Ugh." I should have thought more about how I was going to ask her. "A November due date." I explained, "And we had sex in February." I took a deep breath and let the question roll, "Were you going to even tell me that you were pregnant with my baby?"

"Whoa. Okay, um." She stumbled over a few more words, but none of them were the ones I was hanging on waiting to hear. My eyes were closed as I waited and waited until she said. "No."

My voice raised, shouting, "No? You weren't going to tell me?" Then I took a breath and quieted my voice. "Sorry, I didn't mean to yell. But you weren't going to tell me?"

"What I was trying to say was this isn't your baby, Nico."

I leaned against the kitchen counter and whispered, "But if it isn't, that means."

"That means, my ex and I had one more night together." She explained, "It was after you and I, and," she wavered, "we didn't use a condom."

"Oh," then I questioned, "And you're sure it's his baby?" I didn't know how one would confirm that while they were pregnant, but I trusted she knew how and had done it.

"Yes," she breathed into the phone, "I'm pretty sure."

The racing of my heart calmed, and I was able to breathe easy. "Okay." Then I didn't know what else I should say. "He's probably the better guy for the job anyway." Then I closed my eyes because what was it, a job interview? I tried to joke, "I'm more like the favorite uncle."

"Alright," she took me out of my misery telling me, "I'll talk to you later, I guess."

The disappointment in her voice before she hung up stuck with me more than the relief I felt at finding out the baby wasn't mine. Then instead of celebrating the fact that I wasn't about to be a dad, I was moping around my apartment.

The television was still off, I had a fresh glass of Hennessey in my hand, and I stared at the wall in front of me. I needed to call Nova and share the news, but I couldn't grasp the thought of feeling disappointed. I knew that I didn't want kids, I hardly wanted to have a committed relationship. My life—especially with the traveling—was everything I needed. Outside of being a professional ball player. I was finally good with the way my life was going, I had a new girl often enough, I was traveling, I was making decent money to live it up when I wanted to, and then there was the nagging thought in the back of my head that made me think I wouldn't have been upset if Destiny had my seed growing inside of her.

Then I thought about how my dad was with me growing up and considered if I could be the same. Present, dependable, and reliable. Except I was none of those things. I wasn't lying when I told her I would be a better uncle. I convinced myself that being some kid's uncle was the best I could offer the next generation of Maxwells.

With that, I clicked on Nova's name and dialed his number. When he answered, "So am I going to be an uncle?" My chest heaved before I told him the baby wasn't mine. "Damn. I expected you to be a little more elated. And is that silence I hear in the background? Thought you would have raced down to a lounge to pop a bottle or two."

"Would it be weird if I want to say fuck kids, but I'm also disappointed that I'm not the daddy?"

"Sounds like a question for Maury."

"Who?" I asked with my face twisted up. Nova was always on the same page but a different book.

"Listen, nevermind. You should think about that some more though. Maybe you do want to be a dad, after all. All this time you've been out here trying to fight off commitment, and yet, that's probably the one thing that would satisfy you."

"Whoa. Okay, I think you got me back on track." I laughed. "I'm good, bruh. Next week I'll be back on the road again, back to my grimy ways." I laughed.

"If that's what'll make you happy, bruh, just remember the

anxiety you had with this. Maybe don't fuck *every* chick you meet."

"Yeah, yeah," I told him, "I'll see you at the barbecue tomorrow, and I hope Harmony has invited all her cute friends." I laughed before hanging up and taking the remainder of my drink to the head.

Chapter Twelve

Destiny

After hanging up the phone with Nico, I sat out on Monroe's deck staring at the starter garden she had growing in the backyard. The house she and Alex purchased before they got married was gorgeous. It was a quaint, three-bedroom house in a beautiful neighborhood, with kids riding bikes in the street, and old people waving from their front porch.

She was doing everything to prepare the house to be a home for their future kids. Kids she hadn't had yet, but she knew she wanted. Then there was me, in my one-bedroom apartment still, no man, and a baby on the way who I hadn't started planning for yet. I sighed at the thought of doing it all alone.

I heard the sliding glass door crack open, and Monroe ask, "You still on the phone?" I shook my head and she walked toward me.

I was on vegetable dicing duty before going outside. Monroe

was throwing a barbecue for the holiday weekend, their first since being in their new home. I was over helping her prepare. But when I got the call from Nico, I stepped outside to listen to what he had to say.

Either time I saw him, I didn't suspect he would think the baby was his. What we had was one night, and one night only. We were responsible, despite being frantic, and my desperation to take away the pain from the breakup. We used a condom.

The thought hadn't really occurred to me that the baby growing in my belly could be anyone's but Jensen's. But Nico was right, the math could still add up. My face flushed at the reality I was now living in. I looked to Monroe and said, "That was Nico," softly.

"Oh, how's he doing?" she asked casually, as if it was a friendly call and nothing to be worried about.

My eyes were zoned into the plant, the one that should have borne tomatoes, but the buds were still forming. "He asked if this is his baby." Then I turned to face my belly, growing larger every day. Over the last few months, I imagined what the baby would look like. If he or she would have my features—my eyes, the nose both me and my mom shared, my pouty lips. Or if he or she would have Jensen's. He was a nice-looking man, and his features were pronounced enough to differentiate from mine. His eyes were rounder, his lips thicker, his nose narrower.

Then as Monroe asked, "And what'd you tell him?" I thought of Nico's features, not similar to Jensen's. His skin was darker, he had a dimple in each cheek, and his eyes were wider like mine.

"I told him I'm almost certain it's Jensen's baby." My head fell back, and I felt like I could use a gallon of water. My mouth was consistently dry, and I could never have enough water.

Monroe's hand reached out and she asked, "Can I?" I just

nodded my head as her hand softly rubbed my belly. "Hey you," it seemed she had been practicing her soft, baby voice for months, "I can't wait to meet you. And kiss all over your little face." Then she looked up at me her voice returning to normal when she said, "I think you may need more than *an almost certain*."

"Then what? Either way, the result is the same. Neither dude wants anything to do with *this child*." The baby likely couldn't understand what I was saying, but I only wanted positive energy surrounding them.

"Is that what he said?" My eyes narrowed as I looked at her. "Nico, did he say he would want nothing to do with the baby."

His words were replaying in my head. All the things he said, but I whispered, "No, he didn't say that." Then I corrected, "Exactly. But he also told me he would be a terrible dad."

"So maybe he would want to be there. I mean, the man did call you to ask. He must be somewhat concerned. Wouldn't you rather know for sure, like one hundred percent sure?"

I bit the side of my lip and whispered, "Yeah. I guess I do want to know for sure. Without a doubt." Then I grabbed her hand. "But, Monroe, then what? What if it is Nico's baby, and he wants to be in their life?" The sound of his motorcycle zooming along the highway was my first thought, then of him and all the women he entertains was the second, then I told her, "And now he travels for work."

She scoffed, "Because he wouldn't be the first father in the world to travel for work?" I rolled my eyes.

"Monroe," I pleaded, "I don't know if I need any of this right now." My hand went to my stomach and then I had the urge to snack on something, anything. "Let's go inside, I'm getting hungry."

Inside I returned to my task of chopping vegetables while I snacked on hummus and pita chips. Monroe attempted to distract me, playing music and dancing around the kitchen while she prepared sides—baked beans, potato salad, and macaroni and cheese. "Think any of this will be ready to eat tonight?" I said, looking over her shoulder. "I'll be your taste tester."

She hummed, "Maybe this." She scooped up the potato salad onto a fork. "How does it taste?" The firm potatoes, the mustard to mayo ratio, the onions, and the relish, were delicious but I told her it was missing something. "Oh, maybe more pepper?" She held the shaker in her hand ready to add more.

I shook my head and told her, "No."

The frown on her face made me laugh. "I can't trust your distorted taste buds. I swear that's my niece or nephew in there fucking with me." My eyes widened and we both laughed.

The kitchen counter was covered with containers of food, sauces, condiments, and even the meat that Alex planned to throw on the grill the next day. I found my glass of water and sat at the counter. As much as I wanted the holiday weekend to be the same as the year prior, it was not. I was single, couldn't drink, and then there was the growing belly. I mentioned, "This fourth will be so much different than last year."

Monroe turned from the pan of potato salad and noted, "It will be. New house, husband, *baby bump*." Then she asked, "Are you okay?"

My lips twisted and I let her know, "I am, probably should get home so I can be back here tomorrow to help you set everything up."

Then she reminded me, "Should have just brought a bag and stayed the night." I shrugged. "But alright. I'll see you in the morning."

The apartment was dark and quiet by the time I walked inside. On the drive over, I was convinced the first stop would be the shower and the next the bed. It was neither. I ended up on my couch, my laptop perched on the edge of the couch as I Googled the different ways I could test the paternity of the baby while pregnant.

Blood tests of me and the potential father seemed the least invasive. But it wouldn't be the easiest. Who did I test as the potential father? Nico or Jensen?

Asking Jensen would mean I'd have to explain everything to him, and I wasn't ready for that yet. My mind went into a table of pros and cons, immediately the con side for Jensen was extensive, and I thought it would be easiest to rule out Nico.

Before scheduling, I'd need to know Nico would be okay with taking the test. The back of my couch wasn't the most comfortable place to rest my head, but I did it anyway. My eyes were closed, and I steadied my breathing. None of that eased my thumping heart though. I leaned over the table and grabbed my phone, opening Nico's contact details before gritting my teeth and dialing his number.

I didn't have to wait long for him to answer, in fact, the phone hardly rung. "Need that Icee?" He had a playful tone and I hated to ruin that for him.

"No." I took a deep breath. Talking to Nico used to be the easiest part of my day. Even after exhausting meetings in the office discussing how to revitalize SportsOne's image, or campaigns that were failing despite our extensive efforts, and long nights. I'd end up at his house, a basketball game on TV, and sat beside him with a beer in my hand as we talked about nothing, or everything sports related. "Nico," I paused again. "Your question had me thinking." Then the words were like a river, flowing steadily. "I think I should," I amended that, "We should be sure this isn't your baby."

I could feel the air he sucked in, the silence it left, as I sat waiting on his response. When it finally came, I was at ease. "I think that's a good idea, Destiny. What does that look like though?"

First, I needed to ensure he wasn't upset. "Are you angry?"

He laughed, "Upset that we both laid down in the bed that night and fucked gloriously?" He laughed again, "I'm not a kid, I know decisions come with consequences."

"Okay," I repeated, "Okay, well it'll need both of us to give a blood sample. They'll compare my DNA with yours, and then," my chest rose and fell again, "we'll know."

"We'll know." Then he asked me, "When?"

"I need to schedule it, but I'm hoping as soon as possible."

He explained, "I'm supposed to be back on the road again next week. But I can—" Before he started offering ways he could re-arrange his schedule, I interrupted.

"Right, of course, I should know that." I snickered. "If I can get an appointment for Monday morning, would that work?"

"It would." I was about to tell him goodnight when he asked again, "Sure you don't need an Icee? Or anything?"

This time my laugh came from deep in my belly, likely shaking the baby. "No, I think I'm going to take a shower and climb, slowly, into the bed." He hummed, and the vibration of his voice made me feel something I hadn't felt in a long time. "I'll text you the details as soon as I have them," then I quickly told him, "Talk then." He told me goodnight and I hung up the phone. Just then I felt a thump in my belly, and it was followed by another. I placed my hand to my stomach. "Hey you in there," I whispered.

I didn't want to move, I just wanted to feel the baby, and whatever he or she was doing inside my stomach.

The rest of the weekend went by at a snail's speed—the barbecue, church on Sunday, and the hours after just dragged and dragged. By Monday morning, my eyes were heavy and burning, but I pulled myself out of the bed, dressed, then drove myself to the hospital where I would be meeting Nico for the blood test.

It was one of those days when nothing fit, the sun was shining too bright in the early morning, and even though I used the bathroom before leaving the house I had to pee as soon as I walked into the doctor's office. Nico stepped in front of me though. "Hey," he looked down and asked, "You okay?"

"Yeah," I told him with my head on a swivel, "I just need to use the restroom." I stretched my neck around him. "Over there," I announced, "I'll be right back."

After the pee streamed for minutes, I washed my hands and as the water streamed over my hands, I looked at my face in the mirror—much rounder than it was pre-pregnancy. My nose was wider, my lips even looked fuller. I looked down, grabbed a napkin, and walked out of the bathroom not feeling cute at all. I wanted to get the test over with and on with my day so I could climb into bed. "Good?" Nico was looking at me a bright smile on his face. Nothing had changed on his face—it was still sexy as ever, maybe even more so. "I already checked us in." He pointed to a pair of seats. "They should be calling us back shortly."

My feet crossed and uncrossed as we waited. He was leaning on his thighs, then he looked back to me and said, "That glow." I side-eyed him. "They say pregnant women have a glow. Not sure if I ever recognized it before."

I laughed. "Are you saying this wide nose, full lips, and glossy face is what one would call a *glow*?"

Before he could respond, I heard, "Ms. Harlow," and I stood, with the help of Nico's hand on my lower back. It stayed right there until we were secure in the doctor's office, the nurse instructing us, "Go ahead and take a seat." We were seated side-by-side, Nico's hands rested in his lap. "I'll have a few questions, then we'll go ahead and do the blood draw." I watched as his hands tensed, both forming into firm fists.

The nurse asked her questions, ending with, "Just repeat your birthdates for me." We did. "Alright, who wants to go first?"

"Ugh." Nico looked at me, his eyes as big as saucers.

"I'll go first," I offered. "Maybe you look that way?" He did, immediately turning in his chair to face away from me. I exchanged a look with the nurse, both of us doing our best not to laugh.

The blood draw was quick and painless, and when it was Nico's turn I held my hand out to him. "Here," I told him, "just squeeze." Then I warned, "Just don't break my fingers."

"All done," the nurse announced. "You should have results in a couple of days." She smiled before leaving the room.

The room was sterile, only a single anatomy poster gracing the wall in front of us. Nico was rubbing his arm when I turned to him, "I'll call you, or text you when the results are in."

He turned to me and said, "As soon as you have them." I nodded my head. I understood his urgency in wanting to know. My life had already changed—his was hanging in the balance. The results of the blood test could mean that the two of us would be connected forever, or forever just friends in passing who happened to fuck once.

I wanted to run to the car, despite the fact that my belly wouldn't allow it. Monday morning blues had nothing on the way I was feeling as we walked out of that office. If Nico was the father, that would change everything I had been thinking. Before we fucked, we were at least friends—maybe we could co-parent.

When he stood in front of my car door, helping me get inside, then told me, "Be safe," before winking, it had me feeling some type of way about him. Was co-parenting with benefits a thing?

The results couldn't come in quick enough.

Chapter Thirteen

Nico

Staying in Atlanta would have probably been more appropriate. Sitting courtside watching one of the hottest recruits dribble up and down the court was doing nothing for my nerves, and the interview I needed to conduct was the last thing I wanted to be doing.

My phone was clasped in my hand as I waited for a text or a call from Destiny. Every few minutes I was looking down at the screen just in case the loud noise from the gym disguised the sound of the ringer.

Even in my element I couldn't keep my mind off what was looming over my head. I rubbed my arm in the spot the nurse had to prick for blood. Being a big ass Black man didn't make me immune to the pain of that big ass needle, and it certainly didn't prevent my stomach from getting weak at the sight of blood.

During my stay in the hospital for my condition, it was the

one thing that I couldn't grow used to. Blood draws, IVs—pricking and sticking my body was a no go. Thankfully, most of my monitoring didn't require invasive procedures because my heart literally wouldn't have been able to take all that.

My phone vibrated, and I looked down, but it was only a news notification.

As soon as the kid stopped bouncing the ball, I looked to Jermaine who had been filming B reel for the interview, and told him, "Let's go ahead and get this done." He nodded his head, pulled the camera up, and followed behind me.

"Justin Thompson," I announced as I made my way toward the kid who stood a couple of inches taller than me. "You're looking pretty good out here." His smile that I had been used to seeing in random clips over the season was on full display. "What are you hoping to accomplish this season?"

Justin exchanged a look with me then looked to the camera, or Jermaine, and told us, "I'm looking to dominate the court. Prove to my fans that I'm a worthy player, to the haters that I'm not going anywhere."

I had to laugh because who knew how long he had rehearsed that line, but it was perfect. "And after this season is over, what's next for you?"

Justin was an all-star NCAA basketball player, he'd likely go top ten in the NBA draft if he decided to leave for the league. But his collegiate team was doing well and could be on track to win back-to-back championships. "You know," he held up his hand, "I think I'll take it one step at a time. I don't want to get ahead of myself." He paused and looked at me thoughtfully before revealing, "Nothing is promised, I want to enjoy the season I'm in now, you feel me?"

I could only nod my head because I understood exactly what

he was saying and could likely relate because of other reasons. The advice I left with him, "Do just that. This game has an expiration date on it, don't rush from now to the next milestone because you'll just be rushing to the end."

Justin's mouth opened wide, and he threw his hand in the air to point at me. He looked to the camera and said, "Now that," he laughed, "right there is what I'm living for this season." I nodded at Jermaine letting him know he could stop recording. Justin dapped me up and thanked me for the interview. "Man, really, I know how much you loved the game." He looked down to his feet before looking back to me. "I can't imagine being forced to leave what I love so much."

I assured him, "Prayerfully, you won't ever have that same feeling. Keep doing what you're doing." Then as I told all the kids I encountered. "On and off the court." *All Around* wasn't interested in the athlete that was just dominating on the court, or the field, we were interested in the athletes who were going above and beyond expectations in the classroom or their community too. Justin wasn't the honor roll student, but in his community he was doing his part to inspire younger generations by taking time out to volunteer at the local recreation center.

"I'll do my best," was what Justin said as Jermaine and I packed it up.

"Man," Jermaine said, looking at me, "That guy right there," we were walking side-by-side, "he's something else."

"I couldn't agree more." We were finished for the day, and I was glad I could get back to the hotel room and continue watching my phone for news from Destiny. When Jermaine offered to meet me for drinks I had to decline. "I think I'm calling it an early night, maybe order room service or something," I told him with a slight shoulder shrug.

Jermaine stopped walking and I looked over my shoulder to

make sure he was good. "You've been a little off these past couple of days, what's going on?" he asked, just standing in the entry of the gym.

"I just have some things on my mind," I shared, but didn't plan to give him more details. "I'll be good though." He looked at me carefully and continued walking. I was glad he didn't ask for more details because outside of Nova, I hadn't told anyone about my situation with Destiny. If it ended up not being my baby it wouldn't be newsworthy anyway.

Jermaine and I shared a car, and on the drive to the hotel my phone rang. When Destiny's name popped up on my screen, I thought my heart was stopping. I coughed and grabbed at my chest. Jermaine, knowing about my condition, looked at me and asked, "Nico, do I need to pull over?"

I shook my head, but the coughing didn't subside. The tightness in my chest grew stronger. "I need to take this call," I managed to tell him. As I answered, though, I quickly told Destiny, "Can I call you from my room?"

When she responded, I tried to listen for the tone of her voice for any indication of what she was about to tell me. Her voice was calm, collected, though, not giving any clue to what she had to share.

I massaged my chest as we made our way to a parking spot. Jermaine made sure to check on me again before I dashed into the hotel lobby. "Yeah, I'll catch you in the morning, okay?" I yelled over my shoulder.

I busted through the door of my room and clicked Destiny's number to return her call. The phone hardly rang before she answered. "Okay, I was with Jermaine, needed to get to my room," I quickly explained. Then I asked, "Did the results come in?"

"Sorry to interrupt," she tried to apologize, but I told her it was all good. "And yeah, I have the results." The silence on the line, the time it took her to say her next words, told me all I needed to know. I went to the window of my room and leaned my head against it. The pain in my chest had dissipated, but my head became foggy. I had to listen hard to hear her finally say, "Nico, you're the father." I braced myself against the window, my hand tightening around the phone. "Nico, are you okay?" she asked with a soft voice.

It took me a minute but when I did, it was only to ask how she was doing. "Are you feeling okay?" I took a deep breath. Destiny was carrying my child, it didn't matter how the fuck I felt. "I know this wasn't what you were expecting."

"No," she admitted, "it wasn't." Then she told me, "But for me, nothing changes."

"What does that mean?" I asked, finding a seat on the bedside chair.

"It means that I'll have this baby, and I'll raise him or her." She cleared her throat. "Alone, if I have to."

I wiped my hand across my eyes, holding them closed tight to block out the light of the sun's rays shining through the window. "Is that what you want?"

That question went unanswered. Instead, she told me, "I should give you some time to digest this news."

I hesitated but responded, "Yeah, yeah. I can call you back later, if that's okay." She tried telling me it wasn't necessary, but I told her, "I'll talk to you later."

"A baby," I repeated to myself. Destiny was a sensible woman, stable, and caring. She would probably be a perfect mom—but then there was me.

Trying to process what would happen next, alone, was another reason I would probably suck at being a dad. I called the one person who was much more practical than me.

When Nova answered, he immediately guessed, "It's your baby?"

"How'd you know?" He explained he'd been waiting to hear from me for two days, and the fact that I wasn't hooping and hollering when he answered must have meant I was the daddy. "Yeah, I guess I am not over here celebrating." Then I thought about that and felt bad that I wasn't. "Does that make me a bad dude? That I'm not excited I have a baby coming into the world?" The weight of that thought was heavy on my shoulders. "Shit, man."

Nova started with, "I'm sure you aren't the only guy in the world who isn't excited about their entire life changing." Then he said, "But, this isn't new to you. It's not the first time that you've been caught off guard with a life-changing situation, right?"

"Except this time, it's not just me that will be impacted." I explained, "I could fuck up a kid's life."

Nova laughed, and I had to tell him I didn't find shit funny about the situation. "Whoa, man. You are really fucked up over this, aren't you? Listen. You talk to young guys often, giving them advice, making sure they are making an impact in the community. Do you really think you, of all people, will fuck up a kid's life?"

Standing from the seat, I argued, "Except that's for a few minutes, not on the daily."

"Ah, see, there you go. Already in the right mindset. If you are going to be a decent dad, you must be involved." The tone of his voice dropped as he said, "You can't be a sometimey dad, making do with just a few weekends a month or holidays. You should work it out to be in your child's life as much as possible."

I declared, "Except, Destiny has plans to do it all alone."

"Maybe she thinks she has to." Everything he was saying

made logical sense, but I was feeling it was easier said than done. "This situation isn't ideal for either of you, but you won't be the first or the last to make this work." He told me, "You just have to find a way."

Traveling, the hotel, the happy hour I was skipping to take the call, were all on my mind. I told Nova, "Just when I was starting to enjoy my life, everything is changing." I shook my head. "Again."

He simply replied, "I'm sure she may be feeling the same way."

"Alright man, clearly you aren't up for hearing any alternatives."

"You mean there's something else to even consider?" Hearing him say that made me wish I would have confided in someone, anyone else. "Hey, at least the two of you were cool at some point, not like she was just a complete one-night stand."

The softness of the bed was beneath my fingers as I slid my hand across the comforter. "I guess you're right." I sat down and told him, "Thanks, man."

Before we hung up, he laughed and told me, "You can just call me Uncle Nova now." I grumbled. "Too soon?" The last thing I heard was him laughing as I hung up the phone.

Leaning on my thighs, my phone alternated between both of my hands. I wanted to ease Destiny's mind about me, the least desirable guy, as father to our baby. What that meant exactly was still questionable, and I hoped together we could figure it out.

The phone rang and rang. The first time it went to voicemail, I hung up. The second time, I left a message, "This is Nico. Can you call me as soon as you get this?"

Neither a hot shower nor the replays of game seven were able to release the tension that was building in my shoulders, the headache that had started pounding the back of my head. I needed to talk to Destiny, but my phone didn't ring, not that night.

Chapter Fourteen

Destiny

When I opened the test results and read the ninety-nine percent chance results of Nico being the dad, I had a moment of panic. My plan of not sharing the news with Jensen gave me time to prepare myself before I wanted to figure out a parenting plan. If Nico was the dad, now I'd have to think through what was next.

As his phone rang, my hands were clammy, my heart was beating fast, and I had a cracking voice. Then he had to hang up and call me back. And the time it took for him to return the call had me even more uneasy.

When I finally shared the news, I expected my nerves to settle, but when the next thing that came was a tightening belly, I sat still, my hand rubbing in circles waiting for all the feelings to pass.

It did, then returned a few minutes later. "Shit," I whispered. When it repeated again, I dialed my mom's number. As I waited for her to answer I thought, "I'm only twenty weeks." With twenty weeks remaining, I hadn't packed my hospital bag, hadn't dictated my birth plan. I thought I had time.

When she finally answered, I rushed to tell her about the pains I was having. "Destiny, it's been thirty years since I was pregnant. Ugh," she sounded concerned, "It could be Braxton Hicks." That eased my mind because I had read about those in my pregnancy books. "Or it could be something else, go ahead and call your doctor."

After a couple of questions, the doctor instructed, "Go ahead and get to the emergency room and get checked out." I nodded my head, which was pounding.

I grabbed my purse and called my mom on my way to the car. Leaving my apartment, driving myself, reminded me I was doing this alone and would need my mom more than I thought. "I'm on my way to Piedmont."

"I'll meet you there. Be careful driving, okay?" Driving careful was all I could do because the pains in my head and my belly were all consuming. But I didn't tell her that. I didn't want to freak her out.

It was obviously all over my face when she saw me, though, because she made it her business to yell at the intake nurse, telling her, "She's pregnant and having stomach pains and you are out here asking questions when she should be in there getting evaluated."

"Ma'am, we have to get her information." Then the nurse looked at me, my eyes hardly opened. "Okay, come with me. I'll get the details as we check you out."

"Thank you." My mom placed a hand on my lower back as we made our way to the back.

The nurse hooked up the blood pressure cup and looked at me once it was finished with the reading, "Ma'am, your blood pressure is too high, we'll need to get that down. I'll get the OB on call."

She ran out and my mom grabbed my hand. "Destiny, you're going to be okay. Everything will be okay." As she rubbed my hand, I could hear my phone ringing in my purse. "That can wait," she barked, "but let me turn off the ringer." She dug into my purse, and with my phone in her hand she asked, "Who is Nico?" The blood pressure, stomach pains, and pounding headache didn't need to be exasperated. I closed my eyes and ignored her question. "Right, no need to talk about that now." She placed my phone back in my purse.

A Black woman walked into the room and looked between me and my mom before she assured me, "Try not to stress, you are in good hands with me." She smiled. But stress was the first thing I did when she announced, "It looks like you are dehydrated. Along with your high blood pressure, I think it's best if we keep you overnight for monitoring." The stream of tears started flowing, and all I could do was shake my head. The doctor continued, "We'll get you in a more comfortable room on the maternity floor."

I was wiping my face and nodding my head. Finally, I responded, "Okay, thank you."

My bed was wheeled to the elevator, and my mom never left my side as we rode up a couple of floors. When we were finally settled, she decided, "I'll call Taylor and ask him to grab clothes for me." She moved the phone from her ear and asked me, "Do you need anything? He'll be able to come as soon as visiting hours open in a couple of hours." I shook my head.

While she continued updating Taylor, I grabbed my purse. There was someone else I felt needed an update too. Despite the fact that it was the middle of the night, but I couldn't remember where in the country he was—wherever he was, he was likely sleep.

I called anyway.

"Hello?" His voice sounded groggy, and I knew he was knocked out.

"Hey, sorry to wake you, but just wanted to return your call." I sidestepped telling him I was in the hospital, immediately. I thought giving him a few minutes to wake up would be better.

"Oh, hey." I could hear him moving around. "What time is it?" he mumbled. "I just wanted to," then I heard him shuffling more, "to talk to you about being there for you." He cleared his throat. "And the baby."

I didn't expect him to say that, and obviously neither did my body because the noise on the heart machine started dinging, alerting me that my blood pressure was rising. My mom rushed to the bedside and warned, "You need to be resting, Destiny."

"Hey, is everything okay? Where are you?" Nico asked.

I took a deep breath, watched the machine settle before I told him, "I'm in the hospital." My voice quivered. I felt my mom's hand on my forearm and heard her loud whisper guiding me off the phone. I moved my arm away from her and continued. "Now probably isn't the best time to discuss it."

"Which hospital?" He sounded frantic. I tried to convince him there was no need for him to rush to me, that I would be okay. "Destiny," his voice got a little louder, "which hospital?"

"Piedmont."

"Okay, get some rest," he told me before he hung up.

The beeping of the machines had settled, the only noise I could hear was the drip of the saline from the IV. That was until my mom's questioning started again. I reminded her, "Mom, I should get some sleep." I looked up at her and said, "You should too," then I closed my eyes.

When my eyes opened that next morning, my mom had changed clothes and had a fresh face of makeup, a luxury I was missing. "Good morning," I murmured. "Taylor's been here?" I asked, bringing her attention from her phone to me.

"Good morning, sweetheart. Yes, Taylor dropped off clothes and breakfast."

I smiled. "Thank goodness for Taylor." The thought panged me. Who would I have helping me when the time came that I'd need something? I shook it off and asked, "What's for breakfast?"

Then I heard someone enter the room, and my head turned to see which nurse was coming to check my vitals. I didn't see the nurse, though, instead I saw Nico with a box, flowers, and a worried face. "I brought donuts," he said, walking straight to my bed. "I hope you can eat them."

My face grew into a wide smile as I opened the box, ignoring the proper introduction that was necessary between him and my mom. Not until she rose from her seat and stepped to my bed, opposite of Nico. "Hello." Her voice was stoic. "I'm Ms. Harlow."

Nico looked from me to my mom, then back to me again. "Wow, the resemblance." He smiled at her. "Good morning, Ms. Harlow, I'm Nico." His sentence hung in the air when his gaze returned to mine.

There were a couple of pillows behind my back, and I used those to prop me up. "Mom, this is the baby's father." Instead of looking at my mom for her reaction, I looked to Nico, and the smile that was on his face spread a little further.

"Oh," is all my mom said before she told him, "Well, nice to meet you, Nico. Surprised we haven't met before."

Nico didn't respond to that. Instead, he asked me, "How are you feeling?" Before asking, "Do you need anything?"

"I think I have it covered, Nico. Thank you for coming to

LOVE WASN'T THE GOAL

check on her," my mom replied before I could open my mouth. I cringed and shook my head.

"Mom," I admonished, "Relax."

She grumbled then told us, "I'll give you a minute to catch up. I need to call the office."

With her phone in hand and her purse on her shoulder, she walked out of the room. My eyes closed gently before I looked to Nico. "She can be a little intense sometimes."

His hand reached out for mine, and I let him hold it. "It's cool, I remember when..." He shook his head. "Never mind. I ugh," he stammered, "Do you want me to stay, or should I go?"

"Wait," I paused, "Aren't you supposed to be in the Midwest somewhere?" His exact location failed me but I knew he was on the road for his show. He wagged his head. "You didn't have to come back. I don't even know if I'll be here much longer."

"I wouldn't have been able to think about anything else." He removed his hand from mine, wiping it across his forehead. "There's a lot going on." His eyes connected with mine, and it reminded me that we still had more to discuss. "Right now, I'd just feel comfortable knowing that you are good."

I nodded my head. "I'm good, the doctor should be around soon. Feel free to stick around and hear for yourself."

The side of his mouth lifted. "I'd like that." He looked around the room, a small couch my mom had commandeered and a chair were the only other items in the room. He made his way to the chair beside me. "This floor," he asked after looking to the door, "is the maternity floor, right?" I nodded my head. I could see his chest heaving but he didn't say anything else.

My mother walked through the door and saw Nico sitting beside me. "Destiny, do you need anything?" I shook my head as I grabbed a donut from the box. "I'm not sure you need all that sugar right now." I took a small bite and smiled as I chewed. "Nico," she looked at him, "Mind if we have a word in the hall?"

"Mom," I said again with a long sigh.

Nico raised his hand toward me as he stood. "Sure, Ms. Harlow." He looked to me and told me, "It's cool."

The bed was too far away from the door for me to hear anything that was said. It didn't stop me from trying to crook my neck to listen though. By the time I finished my donut, my mother was walking back into the room. "Where'd he go?" I asked when I saw she was alone.

"I let him know he didn't need to stick around." I sat up a little straighter in the bed, the heart machine beeping as I did. "Destiny, see, that's why you don't need him here."

My mouth hung open, and my eyes were blinking. The table in front of me, holding the donuts, I slid that out of the way as I placed a hand to my stomach. "I don't think my body is responding to him being here right now." I tilted my head. "Pretty sure it's because my mom decided to take it upon herself to dismiss my baby's father."

"Destiny, you need to rest, and not be all worked up." She returned to her couch as if that was the end of it, but I wasn't done.

"What makes you think you have the right to dictate what goes on around here?" Her eyes widened. "I had already told him he could stick around to hear what the doctor had to say." Then I explained how he traveled home to be there, to check on me.

She didn't find any of that admirable, though, and defended it by saying, "If he wanted to stick around he would have."

"Wow," I scoffed. "I can't believe you just said that."

"Besides, a couple of months ago didn't you tell me the baby's father was Jensen?" She threw her hand in the air. "Who is this guy to you anyway? And how did he suddenly become the daddy?" Her face twisted up as she shook her head in disgust.

"It just so happens that it wasn't all of a sudden." I smacked my lips. "Just happened to be recently confirmed."

I didn't know how I felt about Nico being in the hospital. Especially not before we had a chance to talk things over. Despite what he would be in the future, his presence was welcomed, and I was sure to tell my mom that. Her reply, though, "And what does that mean for your plan to raise this child alone?"

Little kicks were felt along my belly, and the feeling still amazed me. I paused to take it all in. "Mom, I know you were a single mom for most of my life, but," I narrowed my eyes at her, "I thought you would want different for me."

She stood from the couch and joined the side of my bed. I moved her hand that was resting on the rail to my belly for her to feel the small kicks. "Destiny," her face was somber, "I do want different for you, but I don't want you to settle for anything less than you deserve." She bent down to my stomach. "Because this child will be loved regardless, and deserves to have the best situation."

"I don't know yet, Mom, but that may be with him in my life."

"We'll see," was all she could say as she continued mumbling to my stomach.

The nurse arrived to check my vitals, and let me know, "The doctor should be here shortly."

Before she left my room, I asked, "Do you think I'll be released today?"

She cringed and told me with a shoulder shrug, "I honestly don't know. Your blood pressure is not in the range it should be, but the doctor can make that determination after examining both you and the baby."

"Okay," I said softly, feeling tears threatening to fall, "Thank you." As soon as she was out of the room, the tears fell. "I need to call my office." My mom returned to the couch, and I called my manager. "I'm still in the hospital," I told her when she asked how I was doing.

"Let us know if there's anything we can do to help, but don't try to rush back here, okay Destiny." I wasn't concerned about work, but I felt relieved knowing my manager wasn't pressed about me returning. "Call us as soon as you know what's next."

"Thanks, I'll do that." I hung up the phone, and although I wasn't going into the office I was still curious about our latest marketing campaign. It featured some of the hosts from the top SportsOne shows, Nico included. I scrolled our social media account and saw his recent interview. I told my mom, "Watch this," as I held the phone out for her to see. "He's not a bad guy," I assured her.

"Hmm," she hummed then reiterated, "We'll see."

I wanted to believe that Nico would be decent, but I knew he was living a fast and furious life. As much as I wanted to trust he'd want to be in his baby's life, he had already warned me that he wasn't the daddy type. I knew well enough to know, if someone tells you something, you should believe them when they say it.

Chapter Fifteen

Nico

"*We got it from here.*" The words were haunting me in my sleep. I woke up staring at the satin blue curtains and gold-framed photos on the walls of my hotel suite. Arguing with Ms. Harlow about being in Destiny's room didn't seem like the best hand to play in the game of trying to convince her I could be there for Destiny and the baby.

As I boarded the plane to re-join my team on the road, I thought about the words, and the underlying sentiment. Ms. Harlow didn't want me in the room, or in Destiny's world. A revelation she probably determined after Destiny gave her a quick background on my life—I was living it with no plans of chilling out.

But there was something so certain in her words, so definitive. I couldn't stop thinking about them. When I made it to Texas the day after leaving the hospital, I called to check on Destiny. Only for her to tell me, "You could have stayed."

I rubbed my face and climbed out of bed. The interview with another top-rated recruit was in a couple of hours, and I needed a couple of cups of coffee to be ready for it.

The stream of hot water on my back helped to ease some of the tension that was building in my shoulders. But the shower did nothing for the thoughts that kept running through my mind. I tried to think of the lady in the lobby when I arrived, the one who checked me in and all but threw her panties in my face.

Her chest was sitting just right, her buttoned shirt hardly able to contain her titties. She wrote her number on the booklet holding my room key. Handing it to me with a wink and a smile, I considered calling her when I got settled in my room. But I didn't. *What the fuck was happening to me?*

I had an hour before I needed to ride to the campus. My next hoop star didn't care that I had a baby on the way, or a woman who wanted to desperately fuck. All he would care about was that he got adequate camera time because the more time he got on screen would up his draft rank—the more people who knew him the better.

That didn't stop me from glancing over at the check-in counter on my way to the café in the hotel lobby. The lady wasn't there though. The woman with the big titties and a cute smile was replaced with a white guy who looked like he would be riding horses in his free time.

"That was a quick trip." I looked up from the floor where I was staring waiting on my coffee to see Jermaine with a wide smile.

"Ugh," I hesitated, "Yeah, a slight emergency, but all is good now. How'd the interview go yesterday?" Explaining that my emergency involved Destiny was not happening.

"Oh, okay." He looked at me then wagged his head. "He's

not you, man." With a laugh, he told me that George, "Can't get into the deep questions like you. He always reverts to the game."

I shrugged. "Guess we make a good team in that way. On the show he's strictly ball, and I'm the *all around*."

He pointed to me. "Exactly." I hadn't planned on sharing my morning with Jermaine, but it ended up being what I needed to get my mind off everything going on back home. "I was thinking that when you went home that maybe," when he paused I thought he knew something about me and Destiny. I didn't know how he would know, but maybe someone had started talking around the office.

"What?" I asked, tapping my fingers on my coffee cup.

"That you had to go to the doctor." My face fell flat, my mouth snuck open. Then he continued, "To check on your heart." As his eyes met mine, he explained, "In the car, before you ran up to your room, you kind of looked like you might have been having a heart attack."

I shook my head heavily. "Oh, that. No." I smirked. "If that was the case I definitely wouldn't have been running." Then I sat back and narrowed my eyes. "If I was having a heart attack you were just going to let me be out here alone?"

He cringed. "Guess you have a point. Damn." He nodded his head. "Glad you are okay though." I looked at my watch and told him it was probably time to roll out. "Should we just ride over together?" I nodded my head. "Cool."

"This kid, of all the kids we've talked to these last couple of months, think he's got it?" I was thinking about his stats from his college career, and they weren't overly impressive. The points he put on the board, when he was in the game, averaged about fifteen. "I don't even know how he ended up on the schedule to be honest."

Then Jermaine told me, "Rumor has it he knows someone

on the marketing team." My head snapped to look at Jermaine as he continued driving.

"On the marketing team? Really?"

"Yeah, like a cousin or something." He tapped the steering wheel and told me he couldn't remember the woman's name. But as soon as he blurted, "Destiny," I coughed. "See, there you go again with that. You okay?"

"C'mon, man," I laughed. "I'm good. Destiny though?"

"Yeah, I think that's her. You know her?" That wasn't something I was ready to explain yet, and I was thankful when he pulled into the parking lot of the athletic center.

The purple and white adorned center, and meticulously manicured lawns, reminded me that we were on a Division One campus. "Every time we end up on a campus, I'm reminded how different these schools are from the HBCU I went to."

"Right," Jermaine said, effectively forgetting the question he had about me knowing Destiny. "I forgot you ended up at an HBCU."

The interview went well, and I was able to focus on Bryan and his star power in the community. Unlike other players I had interviewed, he wasn't doing as much, but what he did do, he made it a point to give it his all. Growing up he didn't have much, so when he was able, he'd volunteer time at the homeless shelter serving dinner. As we were leaving, I waited for Jermaine to start packing up his equipment, and I asked the recruit, "Hey, I heard you know Destiny. She works for the SportsOne marketing department." His eyes went to the ground, and I explained, "No big deal if you do, gotta use what you got to get what you want."

When he looked up to me he smiled. "Yeah, that's my cousin on my mom's side, her dad and my mom are siblings." Then his nose scrunched up. "I was surprised she pulled through, though. I know she's not cool with her dad anymore."

I narrowed my eyes, but Jermaine was moving toward us and I didn't want him to hear the conversation. I wrapped it up with, "Oh, okay." Then told him, "I'll let her know you said hello."

Jermaine and I were walking out of the athletic center when he asked, "Last night in Texas, we living it up or naw?"

"Living it up," I answered, "Of course." On our way back to the hotel, though, I warned him, "I have to change out of these clothes first. I'll meet you in the lobby then we can catch a ride or walk to a bar nearby."

He agreed and when we were back at the hotel we went our separate ways. My phone was ringing and I almost ignored it, but I answered anyway, "Hello?"

It was Destiny and I had been waiting two days to hear an update on how she was doing. "Hey, busy?"

"Honestly," I replied, "I was about to get ready to head out, but I want to know how you are doing."

"Well, I'm leaving the hospital in the morning, but I'll be on bedrest for six weeks." She sounded exhausted and deflated.

"Six weeks?" I repeated as I sat at the edge of the bed. "That's a long time. What's going on?"

"I was dehydrated, and that's good now, but my blood pressure and the contractions have them concerned I could go into premature labor." Then she went on to school me about the baby not being viable yet, and how going into early labor could be fatal for him or her.

All of it sounded terrible, but the only words I could focus on were, "him or her."

"You don't know if it's a boy or girl, yet?"

She laughed and told me, "No, not yet." Then she chastised me, "Is that all you heard?"

"Guess that was pretty bad, huh?" She grumbled. "Right. Six weeks, baby isn't viable." I had heard that too. "And you'll stay at your place for six weeks?" She told me she had plans of staying with her mom and before I could think of the how, I offered, "How about you stay with me?"

"You?" Her voice rang through the phone. "Why would I stay with you?" Her voice sounded as if she was holding back her laughter.

I replied, "Because I want to help." She reminded me that I was on the road and not even at home. "How would that even work, Nico?"

"Ugh, I could come off the road. We have a few more stops on this tour." Which she already knew. "But George can wrap it up on the road, and I can report from the studio." None of which I had vetted with a single soul, and I already knew George on the road wasn't the best look for the show, but that wasn't my problem.

"This sounds hasty, and not planned out. Besides, my mom is here. She has a plan, and I'm sure it'll be fine." The words were coming from her mouth, but she didn't sound confident in them. Not even a little.

"How about you stay with her till I can work this all out, then you come to my place. With me?" Then I added, "It'll be fun." For good measure.

"Fun?" I cringed, because what would be fun about being on bedrest? None of it. I remember when I came home from the hospital and could only do limited activity, it wasn't near bedrest, but it was hell. "How about I give you a call when I'm settled, and eventually we can talk about all of this." Those words sounded even less confident, and her voice was staggering when she said them.

"By all of this, do you mean *all of this*." I had a feeling she was talking about more than her camping out at my place, in the bed. And more about what would happen after the baby was born.

"All of this," she repeated.

"Hey," I blurted before she could hang up, "Bryan said hello." I waited for her to acknowledge him, before I continued, "He's a good kid. What he's doing for that homeless shelter is commendable and should get some eyes on him."

"Yeah, he is a good kid." Her voice was soft and light-hearted. "I knew you'd get around to the good stuff on him."

"And if he wasn't doing all that, would you have wanted to have him interviewed?" I questioned without asking her about their family ties.

"It wouldn't be worth your time if he wasn't doing anything off the court, right?"

I agreed, "Right." Then we got off the phone with a promise that she'd call when she was settled.

After hanging up, I sat on the bed for a while. Then I decided I needed, more than anything, to be out of the room. I changed my clothes and met Jermaine in the lobby. When I spotted him, I tapped his shoulder and said, "Texas won't know what hit 'em after tonight."

Chapter Sixteen

Destiny

My childhood bedroom was the last place I wanted to be. After twelve years, it hadn't changed. Thankfully, my mom did change out the linens, and the fresh sheets with a higher thread count were much more comfortable. Good thing, because my mother insisted that I stayed in the bed, although the doctor stressed I could do minimal movement.

"I can't wait to show your little one this room." My mom was standing in the doorway smiling. "I knew I kept it this way for a reason."

I joked, "Here I was thinking it was because you were cheap and didn't want to remodel it." She frowned, and I remembered I was relying on her for the next couple of weeks. "Sorry," I explained, "being stuck in this room is starting to get to me."

She sat at the end of the bed and asked, "I can help you out to the living room." Then she reminded me, "You have an appointment this afternoon, you'll be able to leave." It had been two weeks since I was released from the hospital, and I still had a month to go. The doctor's appointments were the only time I left the house.

"We should take the scenic route back here." I laughed. Going home was an option, probably not the best option but it was available. Then there was the other option, staying with Nico. He had called every day, a few times a day checking on me, and his offer lingered at the end of each conversation we had.

I hesitated because of obvious reasons, but the more he asked the more I considered it. Bringing it up to my mom was met with disdain though. "Or," I mentioned as she rubbed my leg, "I can take Nico up on his offer." My eyes were set on my stomach as my hand glided over my extended belly button.

"He's offering you a place, but who will cook for you and make sure you have everything you need throughout the day?"

"I haven't thought through all the logistics, but I'm sure I could figure it out."

She pointed at me. "You shouldn't be figuring out nothing right now. You need to be resting and avoiding all stress."

Staying in the bed was partially to allow my body to be at ease, but the other part was to minimize my stress. Thinking about Nico didn't cause me the least bit of worry though. I shared that with my mom and said, "It may be good for us to start figuring out how this will all work once the baby is here."

The exhale that was released from her mouth took me back to my teen years when she'd grow frustrated with me for my random request to be driven to the other side of Atlanta for an event, or when I told her last minute about a project that was due the next day. "Okay, Destiny, if that's what you want, I'll help get you settled over there." Then she tilted her head. "Just know that I will be checking on you while you are there, and he better be okay with that."

I didn't tell her that my heart started racing at the thought of being in his home, or that I couldn't tell if it was the baby kicking or butterflies rumbling around my belly.

She stood from the bed and told me, "Get some rest. I'll check on you in a couple of hours." Instead of closing my eyes and taking another nap for the day, I picked up my phone to message Nico.

Destiny: If the offer still stands, I'll take you up on it.

My eyes were set on the screen, waiting for the text bubbles to appear, but they didn't. Instead, the sound of my phone ringing almost made me drop it into my lap. "Hello," I answered with a smile spread across my face.

"Of course, it still stands. Tonight?"

Then I thought about him being on the road, and I backtracked. "Wait, you are still on the road, right?" As much as he insisted I stay with him, I forgot that he was traveling. A fact that would have been at the forefront had I been in the office. "You still have a couple of weeks on the tour, right?"

"I've already talked to some people, and I can wrap up from the studio." I bit the side of my lip. "I was just waiting on you. I can be on a flight and back home by this evening." My eyes closed tightly. I was throwing all caution, and reason, to the wind. "Hey, don't think too hard about it."

That was exactly how Nico lived life, spontaneously. It was both relieving and nerve wracking. But still, I told him, "Okay. Tonight."

"Great, you know where I stay. I'll check flight details and text you when I'll arrive." Before he hung up he told me, "I hope everything goes well at the appointment today." My mouth was left slightly open because I had only told him once, quickly, about the appointment, and I didn't expect that he'd remember.

"Thanks, Nico." We hung up and I wanted to climb out of the bed and gather all my shit. But that would be more than minimal activity, so I'd have to wait until my mom popped in again to get all that done. I rested my head back on my pillow and let all the what-if scenarios run through my mind until I fell asleep.

"Hey, sleepy head." I heard my mom laughing as she tapped my arm. "Let's get you up and ready for this appointment."

"Okay." I yawned and moved from the bed. My phone fell to the floor. When I picked it up, I saw a message from Nico and read it, *Seven o'clock.* "I spoke with Nico," I told my mom as I walked slowly to the bathroom. "I'll meet him at his place at seven tonight."

"Tonight?" she repeated as she walked behind me. "You sure about this?"

"I know that if all else fails, my childhood bedroom will be right here waiting on me." I turned over my shoulder. "Right?"

She nodded her head. "Always."

Getting out of the house or the ride to the doctor's office should have been the highlight of my day. But not even the news that, "The baby is looking good, and your body seems to be maintaining," could even take the cake. It wasn't until I was walking through the doors of Nico's apartment that my excitement overcame me.

"Hope you don't mind me tagging along to get her settled," my mom said from behind me as she wheeled in my luggage.

"I don't mind at all." Nico grabbed the luggage from her. "You'll be right in here." He directed us to a bedroom. "You'll be in the main bedroom," he told us both, "it's a bit more comfortable than the guest, bathroom isn't too far, and you have big, beautiful windows to look out of." He placed my luggage in a corner and stood beside me. "Should you crawl into the bed now?" Then he laughed, "Sheets are fresh." I walked toward the bed and sat down, not taking the liberty to crawl in quite yet.

"Nico, this is lovely." I knew the tone of her voice, she was about to say something negative. I stared her down and waited for my opportunity to interrupt. "She can't just be here in the bed all day. She'll need help getting around, and she can't cook for herself. How will you do all that?"

Nico looked from mom to me and answered, "I'll make sure she isn't alone for too long, and I can cook." That was news to me, because whenever I visited in the past, he would have a variety of takeout restaurants deliver. But I didn't argue because I needed my mom to be at ease.

"Okay." My mom looked from him to me and reminded me, "Call me when you need me." I smiled and nodded my head. She came in closer and kissed my cheek. "I'll be calling to check on you." It was more of a warning than a loving statement, but I appreciated it the same.

"Ms. Harlow, I'll walk you out," Nico announced, leaving me in his room.

When he returned, I tried to apologize for her, "She's overbearing, sorry about that."

He shook his head. "I suspect that you'll be the same with the baby." He cleared his throat. "Our baby." He was standing in the doorway still, not getting much closer, although it was his room I was invading.

"Nico, I think we should talk about everything." I patted the bed beside me. He sat beside me, and I began, "I honestly did not think it was even slightly possible that this baby was yours. I apologize, I hadn't considered it."

His eyes narrowed and he assured me, "There's no reason for

you to apologize. Hell, until I did a little math, I didn't think it was mine either." He laughed then straightened his face again. "Sorry."

"I went through all my options." I took a deep breath before repeating, "Abortion and adoption, neither of them I could go through with." He didn't speak, just listened. "That left me, and this baby. And I decided no matter what, I'd do it." I explained that my mom raised me alone after my dad left early in life. "And I was convinced that I could do this alone too, if I had to."

I looked to him and his mouth parted. "I get that. But what kind of man would I be if I just let you do that?" He smirked. "I feel bad for telling you I'd be a shitty dad, but I was only speaking my truth." He hunched his shoulders. "I still don't know that I'll be the greatest, but the last thing I'll do is let you do this alone."

My heart doubled in size, and I couldn't stop the tears that had started to race down my face. "Nico," I said to him through sniffles, "I just don't know what any of that looks like."

I felt his hand brush over my thigh. "The more I've thought about it, the more I've realized that I don't think we have to know. Not all of it, not right now."

I wiped the tears that had stained my face. "I'm okay with that."

"Good." He held his hand in the air. "I've been wanting to ask, would you mind?" He looked at my belly.

My face grew into a wide smile. "Of course not." But I didn't expect him to move to the floor, his hands on my belly, his mouth beside it.

"If you can hear me, kick twice," he said, laughing. "This is your daddy." Just when I thought the tears had stopped, there they went again. To make it even better, the baby kicked, not twice, but three times. "Okay, I see you are an ambitious one," Nico said in response.

Shortly after, he stood from the floor and told me, "Now to get you two some food. How does steak and potatoes sound?"

"Amazing." I got comfortable removing my shoes and propping my feet up in his bed. He was right, the expansive windows did give me something to gaze at, and his bed was extra comfortable. I felt like Goldilocks when she finally found the perfect bed. My head rested on the fluffy pillow, and I let my eyes close gently.

That didn't last long though. From the kitchen, I could hear the music. Not that it was a bad selection, the playlist was hitting. But it was loud, I could hear each word of every lyric, the percussion, the piano, the horns, the chorus. I could hear it all. My eyes were wide open, and I was staring at the door thinking if I should say something.

I didn't. I coaxed my eyes closed, eventually, and tried to tune the music out.

The side of the bed compressed, and I peeled one eye open to see Nico placing a tray table onto the bed. "Did I wake you?" He cringed.

"I wasn't asleep." I shifted to hold my head up. "Just resting."

"Here, I brought you some orange juice." He pointed to the glass. "And water," then he told me, "different than the beers we used to drink together."

My nose scrunched. "So much has changed since the times we used to kick it."

He sat beside the table. "When we were watching ball on TV and drinking beers, I would have never thought."

The thought may have crossed my mind once or twice then. But I didn't admit that. "Who would have thought?"

"The food should be finished soon, then if you need help getting ready for bed, I can assist." The smile on his face didn't help hide his intentions.

"I should be okay getting to the bathroom and changing

clothes," I told him, causing his smile to disappear. "It's bad enough that I'm cramping your style staying at your place and needing you to cook for me."

The look on his face when he reiterated, "Cramping my style?" His lips were tight when he suggested, "Guess it would be hard to explain the woman in my room with a very pregnant belly isn't my girlfriend or wife, as I direct them to the other room, huh?" The way thoughts tumbled through my mind, but no words came from my mouth. "Destiny." Nico laughed as he stood from the bed and walked toward the door. "You aren't cramping my style, and I wouldn't bring a woman back to my place."

In the days that followed, I didn't have to worry about that or whether he would be around. He was, every day, back at his apartment right after his show taped, and he'd be there for hours before going back to the office to get ready for the next day.

Even my mom stopped calling every couple of hours thinking I was alone. The thought of being alone raising the baby was no longer a thing—it was how I wouldn't be around Nico on the daily, and that had me sitting in his bed, gazing out the window, with my lips downturned.

Chapter Seventeen

Nico

The bed, the bathroom, then back again. Destiny's time in my house had been limited to so little, and I knew she couldn't move around much, but I was hoping to change up her scenery.

On my way home from the office, I stopped in the party supply store and bought a few decorations. She called out to me as I was putting them up around the living room, "Nico?"

I knew I would be able to decorate without her seeing anything because I don't think she had crossed my bedroom door since she had arrived. I just yelled out, "Give me just a minute."

I stood back and looked at my work. The strings with stars hanging from the ceiling fan, an illuminated moon on the table, dimmed lights, and a platter of wings and vegetables laid out for us to eat.

Destiny was sitting up in the bed when I peeked into the door. "You good?" I asked without going inside. Her belly had been growing even bigger, and her face was starting to widen. But I didn't dare tell her any of that. It didn't matter though; she was still sexy as fuck, even big and pregnant.

Her feet swung over the bed, and she slowly walked to the bathroom. "Think the baby has parked on my bladder," she joked. "Or maybe the baby is also tired of sitting around all day."

I waited for her to return from the bathroom before I announced, "Think you can make it a few more feet?" She looked at me with her head tilted. "Better yet, let me." I went beside her my arms outstretched. "Mind if I carry you?"

"Me?" She laughed. "Nico, I'm not so tiny anymore."

I quickly reminded her, "And I've never been small." I placed an arm around her back, and the other under her legs. "Relax, I got you." Her arm rested around my neck, and I carried her the few steps to the living room.

In the dim light, it took her a few minutes to recognize the decorations. "Nico, what is all of this?" she asked from the comforts of the couch.

"I thought..." I handed her a glass of water, fresh fruit at the bottom of the glass. "You could use a change of scenery." Destiny's tears had become a secondary person in the apartment, making their appearance often. When they started falling down her face, I just rubbed a thumb across them and said, "Those aren't necessary."

"It's just," she sniffled, "you didn't have to do all of this." She shook her head. "You didn't have to do *any of this*." I had a feeling she was referencing more than just the stars, moon, and food, but I let her tell me, "I didn't expect you to be this caring," her eyes blinked, "this nurturing."

With a plate in my hand, piled with wings, celery, and carrots, I said, "You should raise your expectations. If I'm around, you can always count on me to do the most." I winked and handed her the plate. "Besides..." I nodded toward her belly, and she nodded in return, letting me know I could place my hands in my newest favorite spot. "These last twenty-five weeks," my eyes narrowed and she smiled, "you've been holding it down for us."

She sighed, "And after next week, I'll be back to going through life as normal." She wiped her hand on a napkin. "I might miss being spoiled. But really, thank you." We both sat eating wings and watching the illuminated moon take shape in the room.

Destiny had been a welcome guest in my place. Although I had given up my bedroom and had a few mornings I woke up with an aching back, I didn't mind her presence. The thought of her leaving and the apartment being empty again was weighing on me. But then she stated, "I'm sure you are ready to get back to happy hours and hanging out though, right?" And for a minute, the thought of being out and about was exciting. "Yeah, look at that face," she said, nudging me in the shoulder. "I knew I was cramping your style."

"I'm not sure I'll rush back to it actually," I admitted. "The thrill of meeting a new woman isn't there anymore. You know?" Her eyes widened and I assured her, "Besides, me and Trojan have a few things we need to discuss."

She gasped, covering her mouth with her hands. "Nico," she blurted.

I shrugged. "I'm joking." I rolled my eyes away from her. "Seriously though, the thrill of a baby seems to be overtaking the thought of some new..." I stopped myself from finishing that statement.

"Some new pussy? Nico, for real?" She laughed.

"You know honesty is my only policy." But I thought about

the women I had fucked since finding out she was pregnant, and I recanted, "Okay, so the thought of the baby hasn't totally taken over the thought of new, but these last couple of weeks sure have."

"Oh, what, pussy is good until you have to take care of it day and night?"

My eyes widened and I pointed my finger at her. "You know." I nodded my head. "Maybe you are on to something." We both laughed, and she told me at least I'd be off the hook in another week. "It hasn't been that bad though."

"Are you going back on the road?" She shifted, and I asked if she was uncomfortable, then offered to carry her back to the bed. "No," she placed her hand up defensively, "I'm okay."

"I think I may be done with the road," then I added, "at least for now. I have some things here at home I need to be taking care of." I snapped my fingers. "Speaking of which, my mom and Harmony want to throw us a baby shower."

Destiny's eyes went side-to-side before she nodded her head. "That's great." Then she cringed. "How bad would it be that I hadn't considered any of that?" She shared, "Baby clothes, furniture, all that. I should start thinking about that soon."

"Yeah." I rubbed my hands across my napkin. If she had to start thinking about all that, I guess I did too. "Maybe when you are up on your feet, we can hit up a few stores and check some stuff out."

Her plate was emptied, and I asked if she wanted more. "I'm good, actually."

"Good." I eyed the plate. "'Cause you and the kid ate most of it." I laughed. "I'll carry you back to the room." I stood from the couch and got her comfortable in my arms before walking the couple of steps back to the bedroom. I gently placed her at the edge of the bed, but she stood, telling me she was going to hit the bathroom. Before she moved beyond me, though, her eyes met mine and I let the stare linger for a minute too long. I had to shake my head and move aside because the thought of kissing her was overwhelming.

I turned to face the bedroom door and told her over my shoulder, "I'm going to get everything cleaned up then watch the game. If you need me, let me know." I walked out without turning to look her way again.

"Thanks, Nico," I heard her say as I walked out.

I heard the shower turn on, and the thought of her climbing under the stream of water naked had me wanting to return to the room. The moon was still shining and the stars floating from the ceiling fan. I quickly turned on the lights and flipped on Sports-One. I needed to get my mind off Destiny, and her naked body, and onto something else. The game was doing it until I heard Destiny shout, "Nico, can you help?" Then the shower water shut off.

I went to the bathroom door and yelled, "What's up?" After she explained she forgot a towel, I knew I would have to walk into the bathroom to grab it for her. "Ugh, and you want me to come in?"

"Please, I don't want to slip trying to get to it."

My hand went to the doorknob, then I closed my eyes. Quietly saying to myself, "Chill man, the fuck?" To get from the bathroom door to the linen closet, I had to walk directly past the shower where Destiny was likely standing, naked, dripping wet. But if I turned the other direction, she'd still be there, in the reflection of the mirror. So, I opened the door, focused my eyes to the ground and walked, quickly.

I grabbed a towel, turned and did the same thing on my way back. There was only one problem, I'd have to look at her to get the towel into her hands. "Here you are," I said, looking at her then trying to look away. My eyes were stuck though. Her body, as sexy as it was before, the bare belly, was, "Damn, Destiny," I mumbled.

She wrapped the towel around herself. "I know, it's a lot, right?" She and I were not on the same page, or even in the same damn book. "All those stretch marks." Which I didn't even notice. "My belly button, who knows if that will go back in." I couldn't care less about that either.

"Destiny," I licked my tongue across my lips. "I better get out of here." I walked to the door and closed it behind me. Watching sports highlights wouldn't do, and the guest bedroom wasn't far enough from the thoughts I had running through my mind. I needed a release. Bad.

In the guest room, I grabbed my own towel and made my way to the hall bathroom. Hastily undressing, I hopped in the shower. The warm water streamed down my back and one hand went to my dick that was already standing at full attention, the other hand to the wall as I braced myself for the tension that was built up.

My hand stroked, and stroked, until I felt my eyes clenching tight and my body jerking, all the while the only image in my mind was that of Destiny's naked body—big and beautiful.

I climbed out of the shower, towel cloaked over my waist, then I made it back to the living room to turn off the television. After, it was to the guest bedroom where I laid in the bed staring at the ceiling thinking about Destiny. *Fuck.*

My phone dinged, and it was a message from her.

Destiny: You okay? In bed early tonight.

"No, I'm not. I would rather fuck you than rub one out, but

fucking is probably prohibited on bed rest," was what I really wanted to say. The fact that she was just in the other room had me wanting to respond in person. I kept it cool though.

Nico: Yeah, I'm good.

But it took me hours to finally fall asleep.

Chapter Eighteen

Destiny

As badly as I wanted to leave my childhood bedroom at the beginning of bedrest, I was sitting on the edge of Nico's bed thinking there was something so comforting about his place I didn't want to leave. But being up on my feet, back in my own space, and catching up with my girlfriends had its appeal too.

I had one more day, and another doctor's appointment, before I was cleared from bedrest, but I managed to carefully pack up my bag. The energy it took to do that had me leaning against the side of the bed, my hand on my stomach when Nico came into the room. He took one look around and asked, "Was your mom here?" I shook my head. She had been making random visits, but not that day. "Who packed your bag?" he said, his eyes not leaving the zipped-up luggage in the middle of his floor.

"Oh, I just had to put a few things inside, it wasn't too bad," I explained.

"Hmm, I'm not sure your mama would agree with that." He laughed. "And I probably would agree with her." I had stopped being shocked at what he had been sharing lately. Nothing about Nico was what I expected anymore. Something about him was changing on the daily.

"Alright, good thing I'm feeling fine then because I'd hate to have to hear it from either of you otherwise." He nodded his head.

"I brought some soup and salad for dinner." He pointed to the bed and directed, "Get comfortable. I'll bring it in."

I wanted to tell him I could join him in the kitchen, but considering I was already pressing my luck with my luggage, I sat my ass down on the bed and waited. He came back carrying the dinner tray, and on it there was a bowl, a plate, and a vase full of flowers. "Aw." My mouth opened wide. "That's so sweet."

He hunched his shoulder and placed the tray in the bed beside me. He left out then returned with his own bowl and plate. "I'm not going to lie, I will like being back in this comfy ass bed."

I frowned because that was one of the things at the top of my list that I'd miss. "I'm def going to miss this bed." Then I teased, "May have to get the details on this mattress for real though."

"I got you," he promised, and that phrase had become a regular one he threw out without even thinking about it lately.

"You'll be back in the office after tomorrow, right?" he asked as he blew the soup on his spoon.

"Yup." And because I hadn't been to the office in a while I asked for an update. "How has the show been going, is the team keeping you all hitting your numbers?"

"Seems like they have been doing alright. I haven't heard my team complaining, so I guess so." Then he told me, "I shouldn't have asked about the office, though. You still have one day to remain stress free. Forget about that shit." He laughed.

"And you know what? I think I will." Each weekend for the past month, we had both been in the house, Nico popping in and out, but for the most part he was right there. "Plans for the weekend?" I asked, trying to figure out what I'd do with my own time.

His eyes went to the ceiling, and his lip curled up. "Haven't thought about it really. You?"

"Same. Haven't really thought about it."

"If you can't find anything, maybe we can go out, or something," he said that so nonchalantly, but something about it felt more than just a random hangout.

"Or something," I repeated, my eyes on him when I asked, "Is that a casual or something, is that a 'we are about to be co-parents' or something, or?"

"It's what you want it to be, honestly." Then he told me, "I'll take your dishes." He stood from the bed and collected everything before he disappeared. I turned my head toward the window, and that's where they were when he returned to the room. I felt his hand on the side of my face. "Destiny," he said, making me turn my head toward him.

He leaned down and before any more words could be exchanged, his lips were on mine. His lips soft, his tongue prying, his hand caressing the side of my face—and I sunk into it all. My hand reached up to cup his face, pulling him closer to me, as close as he could be from the side of the bed. Then as my body began to respond, my nipples hardening, my pussy throbbing, I moved my hand to his chest and gently pushed him away.

He was breathing hard, his eyes half closed as he looked at me. "My bad."

I shook my head. "If this wasn't all happening how it was, I'd want all of that and a lot more. But..." I looked at him, my eyes going to his full lips. "With all of this going on," one hand gripped my belly, making my mind focus on the baby and not the sensual feelings, "I don't think it's a good idea for us to confuse things."

His eyes narrowed. "There's no confusion on my end at all." He wiped his hand across his mouth. "I want you, bad." I wanted to tell him the feelings were mutual, because fucking him was something I thought of every night as I laid in his bed, the scent of him permeating my senses.

"It could end all wrong. Right now, I think we'll be able to do this. Whatever it is. However we try to make it work." My words were stumbling out of my mouth, trying to beat the pace of my racing heart. I released my hand from where it was still resting on his chest.

He looked at me and stood tall, nodding his head. "Maybe you're right," he told me before walking out of his bedroom.

That night was no different—I thought of that kiss, and how many different ways I wanted to feel him all over my body. The next day, though, I left his house for my doctor's appointment knowing that the next fourteen weeks, I wouldn't have the luxury of being spoiled by him, or haunted by his scent, his bed, his company.

That weekend, I spent the day moping around feeling the loss of all of that. It wasn't until Monroe called, warning, "I haven't had the chance to hang with you in six weeks, we are going to brunch," that I let the thoughts leave me.

I sat across from her pouting. "What is brunch without endless mimosas anyway?"

She tipped her glass toward me and replied, "I hope I won't

know for a couple more years, at least." Then she took a sip from her glass. "I'll drink a few for you." She winked. "Tell me, how was bedrest?"

At least the food was on point, making up for the fact that I couldn't drink. "If not leaving a bedroom for weeks is your type of fun, you would have loved it." I smirked. "It was terrible."

"But bitch, you were with your fine ass baby daddy." Then she lowered her voice and looked over her shoulder. "Don't tell Alex I said that, okay?" We shared a laugh.

"We were together, but I don't know if that was a good thing or not." I knew that giving her too many details would have had us on the topic for too long, so I tried to make it as bland as possible.

She caught on though, asking, "Not once did the two of you do more than share space?" I grabbed my glass, filled with orange juice only, and sipped. "Oh yeah, you need to spill it."

"There were a couple of tense moments." I laughed. "Girl, I had to have him bring me a towel." I explained how I was standing there, butt ass naked. "And he couldn't even look at me." I shook my head.

"He couldn't?" She narrowed her eyes. "Or he didn't?"

I hunched my shoulders. "He didn't. Actually, he did, but then he scurried out of the bathroom quickly." Then I thought about that night and how quickly he went to bed. "He even went to bed right after."

"Oh, you had him hot and ready. Poor man." She laughed and I thought about it, my nose scrunching as I realized she may have been right. "And that's it, just a glimpse of your naked body?"

"There was a kiss." I explained, "A hot and heavy kiss. But I told him we couldn't go there."

"And why the fuck not?" Monroe was never the one to hold anything back.

"Girl, because," I rolled my eyes, "if we are going to be co-parenting, then we shouldn't blur the lines. It was one thing to fuck and go on about our business, but to fuck, sometimes, then have to drop the kid off other times." I shook my head. "No, I don't want that." Then I explained, "And what if one of us decides to get in a relationship, or wants to stop fucking, then what? How easy will it be to keep it moving?"

Monroe tapped the table, interrupting my spiraling thoughts. "Let's be real. Having a baby is going to be challenging for your dating life. And co-parenting with someone like Nico Maxwell, is going to add some additional complexities. But," she frowned, "I get it. Maybe it would be difficult to mix pleasure with parenting." She quirked her head to the side then sighed deeply.

"Ugh, you are making me dread all of this." I plucked at the napkin in my lap.

"Alright, no need to dwell on those things." As if her next topic was even better, she asked, "What's up with Jensen, seen him lately?"

"No." I shook my head and looked around at the tables nearby. Everyone seemed to be enjoying unlimited mimosas, chatting it up with their friends, and there wasn't a single table there with kids. Not a single one. "I suspect he's somewhere around the city living his best life." Once I determined that Nico was the father, I hadn't thought much about Jensen.

"Hmm," she hummed, "Wonder what he would say if he saw you right now."

"Let's hope that you are not conjuring up a situation right now." I side-eyed her.

"Atlanta isn't that big, you know." She tipped her glass up

again and continued enjoying her mimosa. "Anyway, now that you are closer to the finish line, I'm sure it won't happen before the baby is here. Then there's no issue. Maybe he'll just see you out with Little Maxwell and not think anything of it."

I laughed, "Little Maxwell?"

"Until you give me a name to call my niece or nephew, it will be Little Maxwell to me," she said confidently.

"You'd think six weeks on bedrest, not able to work and hardly move I would have started planning some shit out. Like a name, baby items, a plan with the baby daddy." I clenched my lips then said, "Nothing. Nada. Zilch."

"Don't worry, I'm not too far removed from my planning days. Planning a wedding is about the same, right? Shower, organization, getting people where they need to be when they need to be somewhere." She reached across the table and patted my hand. "Auntie Monroe has this covered." Then she tilted her head and asked, "Now how involved do you want Nico to be in the planning? Like, is he able to give input on the name, or naw?"

"Input, sure, will I have a junior, no." Her eyes widened. "It's never been my thing." I paused. "Even when I thought Jensen and I would get married, I would joke that we'd have a gang of kids, but none of them would be a junior, and none of them would share our initials."

"Okay, so that eliminates Daysia." I squinted my eyes. "What? I love that name."

With a hand rubbing across my forehead, I told her, "No. Just no."

Our plates were cleared, although I think Monroe would have stayed longer. When it came to an *unlimited* option, she had a five-drink minimum and she was only on drink three. "I'll drop you off," I offered.

"Sure."

As we were walking out of the restaurant my phone vibrated. I pulled it out to see Nico's name across the screen. Since leaving his house I hadn't spoken to him. It felt weird to go days without speaking, after spending most of our days doing just that. I answered, "Hey, Nico."

Monroe grasped at my arm. "Nico," she whispered loudly, and I just nodded my head and continued walking to the car. As soon as we were ready to pull off, the phone connected to the Bluetooth and Monroe announced herself. "Hey Nico, this is Monroe, I'm in the car with Destiny. She's giving me a ride home." As she continued, information just falling from her mouth, I turned and looked at her. "Oh," she mouthed as she clamped her jaws shut.

"Alright, what's up, Nico?"

"I didn't mean to disturb you. Glad you got out the house though." Then he lingered and Monroe stared at me with her arms in the air.

"Me too."

"Do you have plans for the rest of the day?" My hands circled the steering wheel and I tried not to glance over at Monroe.

"No." I heard her clapping her hands together softly. "I just planned to be at home getting some stuff done around the apartment.

"Mind if I come through?"

I choked. "Come through?" I cleared my throat. "To my place?"

"That's where you said you would be, right?"

"Sure, yeah. You can come by. I'll send you the address."

As soon as I hung up, Monroe burst out into, "Hell yeah. He's coming to collect some of that pregnant poonani."

I groaned. "No, we'll keep it cordial."

"Believe that shit if you want to," she blurted as I pulled up to her building. "Thanks for the ride, mama." She blew a kiss. "I'll call you later to hear all about your experience. If it's good, good, I may have to move up that window on them babies." She laughed as she climbed out of the car.

Chapter Nineteen

Nico

Nova usually frequented my apartment. At least once a week he was there watching the game, drinking beer. It was rare that I went to his place, especially since he was living with Harmony. I didn't want to disrupt their flow. I needed to talk to him, see his face when I asked him the question, so I was standing on the front steps of their newly built house. One that could have easily housed a family of ten.

My hand was raised to the door, knocking, when I finally heard someone shuffling down the hallway headed my way. "Nico?" Harmony answered the door, eyes squinting, as she looked up to me.

"Good morning, sorry, were you asleep?" I asked, looking down at my watch. It was after ten in the morning. "Long night?" I joked, knowing that Harmony and Nova didn't go out much.

"I was sleep." She nodded her head and moved out of the way

for me to walk through the foyer. "Had to test a product after hours last night." She yawned. "Nova might be in the living room," her hand flapped in that direction, "or kitchen. I'm sure you'll find him." She trekked back up the stairs and left me to myself.

I walked through the house carefully, looking in their office first, then moved to the back of the house to the kitchen and living room where I finally found Nova—his laptop resting on his legs, the news on the television. "This is what Saturday mornings look like for a married man?" I asked, tapping him on the shoulder.

"Nico?" He looked up from his laptop. "What's up? You good?" He stood and stared at me. Nova had a habit of checking on me, more than necessary, as if he had the ability to diagnose any illnesses I had going on.

"I'm good." I wagged my head. "Kinda." His eyes narrowed and he told me to take a seat beside him. Before I started talking, I looked around the house. I hadn't been there since they first moved in, and I had to admit the place was starting to look good.

"I like what you two are doing with the place. Is that Harmony or you?"

He smiled slightly and shook his head. "That's all Mom." I nodded knowingly. Our mom had an eye for interior design.

"I'll keep that in mind." I knew I had a guest room to convert. "Anyway, I have a problem." I sighed.

My problems usually involved my health, or some random ass adventure I signed up for. If I was talking to Nova about it, it hardly ever had anything to do with a woman. I wasn't surprised when he guessed. "You don't look like you are sick, so you are hiking a mountain, running a race, swimming with sharks?"

I shook my head. "First of all, no." I just stared at him. "Bruh, swimming with sharks though?" Then I continued, "It's Destiny."

His eyes widened because her health was as much a concern to him as my own. When I told him she would be on bed rest, for six weeks, at my house, I had to stop him from wanting to come to check on her every couple of days. "Is she okay? She's off bed rest now, right?"

"She is, she left a few days ago." The reminder made my gaze turn toward the ground.

"Ah, that's it." He put a hand to my shoulder. "You didn't want her to leave, did you?"

My eyebrows bunched. "That's not it. I didn't mind her leaving. I'm sure she wanted to be back in her space. But it's just that, I feel for her more than just a baby mama."

He smirked. "Man." He stood from the couch and faced me. "Listen, if you are about to tell me you want to fuck your baby mama, I'm going to tell you don't do it."

My nose scrunched up. I didn't exactly like the way he phrased it, but it was exactly what I wanted to do. And I suddenly remembered why I left out topics about women when we talked. "Don't do it?" I questioned, staring up at him.

He shook his head intensely. "Tell me the last relationship you had." His arms crossed over his chest.

I easily knew the answer but still argued, "Why does that matter?"

"Because you don't do relationships. You fuck." He looked toward the front of the house then lowered his voice to say, "And not only do you fuck, you fuck and leave. Do you really want to mess things up with the woman who will be raising your kid?"

"Man," I sighed. "Okay." I held my hand up. "What if I was in a relationship with her?" The thought sounded foreign because my last relationship was back in high school, and that was only because she thought fucking made us a couple, but that didn't last long.

The way he laughed, loudly, had me frowning. "Nico, you in a relationship?" I shrugged. "What kind of voodoo magic was she working while she stayed with you?"

"I'm glad you find all this funny, but I'm serious." I sat back on his couch, pulling a pillow into my lap. "Destiny said she wouldn't want to cross the line because it would confuse things. And I get that, fucking then going about my business would fuck some shit up. But if we were together, like a normal ass couple, having a baby."

"You mean, not like one that fucked once and the condom broke?"

"Man, damn." I threw the pillow to the couch and stood up, my chest heaving. "I'm serious."

"Alright, then be serious. Talk to her." He hunched his shoulder. "Tell her what you want, and prove to her that you can do what you've never been able to do before. Commit to one woman."

"You were able to do it," I taunted.

"Two sides of the same coin." He shook his head. "If you see it like that, I'll be happy for the two of you." He raised his hand in the air. "Just know I warned you. You fuck this up, things could become exponentially harder for you in the future."

I tapped his chest. "You know what I love?" I tilted my head to the side. "A good challenge." I looked to his kitchen and asked, "What's for breakfast?"

Then I heard footsteps in the hallway. "Did you say you were cooking?" She leaned onto the counter and rubbed a hand across her face.

Nova was drawn to her like a moth to a flame, rubbing her back as soon as he reached her. "You want breakfast?" She nodded her head. "I got you." But instead of whipping out pans and opening the fridge, he grabbed his phone. "Nico, you staying?"

"Might as well." I smiled.

"What brought you to the house on a Saturday morning anyway?" Harmony pulled out a seat at the counter and turned to look at me.

I joined the two of them in the kitchen. "I needed some brotherly advice." I side-eyed Nova. "But this hating ass dude."

Harmony buckled over laughing. "Wait, what?" She looked between the two of us when she sat back up. "What'd you ask?"

That's when Nova interjected. "Basically, he wants to fuck his baby mama." Harmony's mouth dropped open.

"What's the shocking part?" I looked at Harmony. "That I want to fuck, or that I want to fuck her?"

"I don't know *all your business*. But what I do know is that you aren't a repeat offender, right?" She looked at me, her eyes assuming. "I'm going to guess Nova told you that's a no go, right?" I nodded. "Good, because that's what he should tell you. Why would you want to make things complicated?"

I smacked my lips. "Not you too, Harmony." Her eyes went from side-to-side. "He left out the part where I said I want to be with her."

"With her? Like a relationship?" I nodded. "Oh, wow." Her eyes opened a little wider. "In that case, I hope it works out for you two." She looked at Nova and told him, "I mean, that would be the best situation for all involved, right?" Then she sneered, "But have you ever been in a relationship?"

"Ugh," I groaned. "Here we go." We all laughed.

By the time I was leaving their house, I had convinced the two of them I was capable of being in a relationship. It was time to convince the only person who really mattered though.

I hadn't heard from her since she left my place, though, and I was giving her space to adjust to being out of the bed. That afternoon, though, I was ready to reconnect. When I dialed her number, and I heard her friend in the background, I almost reconsidered what I wanted to say. But when she accepted my offer to hang with her, at her place, I was geeked.

In the years of hanging with her, it had always been at my place or some mutual location. Never her place. On my way over, I stopped at the grocery store and picked up flowers, and a couple of snacks.

Her apartment building was a lot like mine, and not too far from me. Taking the elevator felt a little different though. We had just spent weeks together, sharing the same space, talking about random shit—but going to her place wasn't the same. The elevator doors opened, and I looked down at the flowers in my hand, the bag of snacks I was toting, and walked carefully to her door.

She didn't make it to the door quickly. I looked at the numbers plastered on it, thinking maybe I was knocking on the wrong apartment. Or maybe she wasn't home. I started to dig my phone from my pocket when the door opened. "Oh, hey." I looked at her and smiled. "Guess getting around takes a little more time now, huh?"

She winked and moved out of the doorway, slowly. "I think my feet are protesting after being propped up for weeks at a time. I probably should have eased back into a routine." She twisted her face, but it eased when I held up the flowers.

"For you." Then I looked at her belly and tilted my head for her to nod. I leaned down and whispered, "And for you," before placing a kiss on her belly button. She laughed before I stood, holding up the bag for her to examine.

"Oh, what's in there?"

"Chips, cookies," her eyes were growing wider as I continued, "And your favorite chocolate bar." I pulled that out first.

"I probably should be careful with all the junk food." She gritted her teeth then reached her hand out for the Hershey's bar with almonds.

I moved in the direction of her kitchen and asked, "Should I hide this somewhere up high then?" She laughed and called me an ass as I reached on top of her refrigerator, opening the cabinet there to stuff the bag inside. "Just call me when you want to take it down."

"Even if it's in the middle of the night?" She had already ripped open the wrapper of the Hershey's.

"Especially if it's in the middle of the night." I peeked around the wall of the kitchen and wriggled my brows.

Only for her to sigh. "Nico."

Her lips were puckered, and I wanted nothing else but to kiss them tenderly. Instead, I let my lip rest between my teeth and walked out of her kitchen. "Okay, how about you give me a tour of the place?"

I could see the kitchen and the small dining table beside it, the living room with large windows, then a hallway that led to the rooms, I assumed. "There isn't much to see," she said, walking slowly in front of me. I followed behind her anyway. "The bathroom," she pointed to her right, "And the bedroom," she pointed straight ahead.

"One bedroom?" I asked.

When she told me, "Before recently, it was big enough." She led me back to the living room where she sat on the couch and propped her legs up on the coffee table in front of her. "Amongst other things, I'll need to move into a larger apartment." I asked when her lease would be up and she answered, "A couple of months after the baby is here."

The only thing I could think of was the large house Nova and Harmony had. One that could fit a family of three easily. "Are you thinking about another apartment? Or?"

"A house?" She shook her head. "I wish I was better prepared to move into a house right now." Her fingers started picking at her leggings. "Jensen was the practical one, he was saving, I'll admit," she adjusted slightly on the couch, "I shouldn't have depended on him as much as I was."

Her head rolled back, and I hated that he was the topic of discussion. "If only we all had the ability to predict the future." I smiled softly and let my hand rest on her thigh. "Is this okay?" I asked.

Her eyes met mine, and she nodded her head. "Yeah," she said, her voice sounding raspy.

"Me and Jensen have one thing in common, and from what I can tell, only one thing." I looked at her intently. "I have my shit together too." Then I asked, "Can you not hold him against me? Let me prove that's the only thing we have in common."

"Jensen didn't want to marry," she cleared her throat, "me. And as much as I know about you, you aren't looking to get married either." Her eyes left mine.

My fingers tapped against her leg. "I don't even know when things started changing." I watched my fingers against her leg. "Had you asked me a few months ago what I was doing with my life, I would have told you it was," I started singing, "Fuck bitches, get money." Then I snickered, "Not even the get money part, but you know what I'm saying."

That probably wasn't the best reference. Destiny's eyes were as wide as saucers when she looked at me and said, "The baby."

I shook my head and said, "No, Lil' Wayne." She pointed to her stomach, and I squinted.

"The baby." She pointed to her stomach again. "You know you'll have to watch your mouth when the baby is here, right?"

"Are you telling me the baby will come out screaming, 'get money'?" I laughed. "Okay."

She rolled her eyes. "Anyway. What happened? What's changed?"

"You." The answer was simple, because after thinking about it, it wasn't even the baby. It was Destiny. "I could have been denying it before, when we were just kicking it." I laughed. "But then we fucked, and," my eyebrows arched, "and now seeing you handle your shit. Despite whoever and whatever else, that shit did something to me." She laughed. "You laughing. I'm serious."

"You are telling me you aren't on any of that anymore?" I shook my head, and she smirked. "But it wasn't just the women, despite them being numerous." She noted, "You out here living like Evil Knievel."

I thought about what she was saying. Then I looked at her and asked, "Would that bother you?"

"It should bother you."

"Hmm," I hummed. "Maybe, I feel you."

Chapter Twenty

Destiny

I wanted to be with Nico, more than anything. If we could make it work for our little family, that would be the most ideal situation. After he admitted he had changed, I was willing to give us a chance. I didn't let him know that then though. I needed to think about it, without him being in my face all fine and fuckable.

In the middle of the week, I woke up and decided it was time. Time to let him know I was ready. Before the baby, a mid-week, after-hour event would have been nothing. I don't know what I was thinking doing that shit twenty-eight weeks pregnant. Energy hit a little different.

I knew I wouldn't want to navigate the grocery store, so I went ahead and had them delivered. I had texted him the night before and asked him to meet me at my house after work. As soon as I got there, I changed out of my business casual into something more casual—I wish I could have rocked something sexy, but the way my belly was setup, that was an epic fail.

The dinner I planned to cook was baked lasagna, garlic bread, and a salad. Easy enough. Except I pulled the ingredients out and immediately needed a break. I sat on the couch and propped up my feet, and that's where I was seated when I heard the knock on my door. "Shit," I mumbled as I made my way over to open it.

When Nico walked inside, he sniffed the air and said, "Are we eating?" I twisted my face and looked to the kitchen. "Do you need help?" He followed me into the kitchen, where all the ingredients were still on the counter. "Or you need me to cook?" He laughed. "What happened?"

I looked down at my belly and explained, "I intended on cooking you a fabulous meal." I licked my lips. "I was craving lasagna, but I needed a break before I even started."

His hand went up to my face, and he smiled. "If I knew how to cook lasagna, I'd whip it up." He fumbled in his pocket and held his phone up. "What I can do is order it though." He started tapping away on his phone then said, "It'll be here in thirty." He grabbed my hand and walked me to the living room. "How about you just relax." He sat beside me and pulled my feet into his lap, massaging each one.

As he did, I told him about my grand plan for the night. "You were supposed to come over here, candles would have been lit. I would have had the food in the oven, Italian seasonings filling your senses. Making your mouth water." I plucked at the oversized shirt and leggings I had on. "And this would have been a sexy little dress." My nose scrunched up. "Just imagine all that, okay?"

He licked his tongue across his lips. "And why would you have been doing all that?"

"It would have been the perfect setup to tell you…" His

thumb massaged a sore spot in the pad of my foot. "Oh." I took a breath before telling him, "It would have been to tell you that I want to give us a try. Maybe date, see where things go." My finger moved to the side of his ear.

"I like where this is going." Then he asked, "Are we imagining anything else?" His hand massaged up my calves. "Like what is happening after dinner?"

"Oh, that." I leaned closer to him, as much as my belly would allow. "I don't think we need to imagine that part." His face turned toward mine. "We can make that a reality." Then I told him, "These days I've been feeling dessert before dinner anyway."

"Wait." His hands left my legs and went into his pocket, then he pulled his phone out again. He was tapping, even faster than when he was ordering the food, and I waited, trying not to look at his screen. "Okay." He was nodding his head. "The internet is saying you can have sex throughout your pregnancy." He looked up and smiled at me. "Even now." Then he leaned closer to me and whispered, "Is that what you want? You want to have sex with me now?" I wagged my head. Before he moved closer, he asked another question, "Sex before a first date?"

I laughed and told him, "I mean, we crossed *that* bridge a while ago."

"Ehhm." He stood from the couch. "I guess you are right." One arm went under my legs, and the other behind my back. "Hold on tight," he instructed as he walked me to the bedroom. As he laid me down on the bed, he said, "This is a first." His eyes were on me like I was a buttered roll, fresh out the oven. He leaned down and tugged at my leggings—the fact that they had the material covering my belly had me clenching my eyes closed to avoid watching that hot mess. Then they felt like they were suctioned to my body, and it took him some time to roll them down my legs. I was thankful he persisted.

When he reached up, his hands grazing my belly, I moved to the side, letting him pull my shirt over my head. I was laying there in my maternity bra and panties, full belly out, and still he said, "I want to remember you, just like this, forever." My eyes popped open and looked at him before a tear rolled down my cheek. "You may not feel it, but know this body is gorgeous." He kissed between my boobs, then down the side of my belly before he kneeled down at the edge of the bed.

"I should tell you." His head was between my legs, and I wanted his mouth to be moving, but he could have saved the words. When he told me, "That site said that pregnant women are overly horny." My eyes looked down at him and my eyebrows raised. "Hmm, let's see about that." He tugged on my panties, dropping those to the floor.

I had to maneuver my hips for him to reach my pussy, and when he did, "Oh God," rolled out of my mouth effortlessly. It could have been the pregnancy, or the fact that it had been months since the last time I was touched, there, sexually. Whatever it was, the way his tongue was finding new crevices, hidden by my growing belly, had me wanting to make more babies with him.

His finger grazed against my clit, as his mouth kissed my thighs, and all of it had my senses heightened. I wanted to grab him and drag him between my legs, but I let him continue his quest instead. What he had in store for me was far better than anything I had been imagining the past couple of months.

Then he held the bottom of my foot and rested it on his shoulder. As he licked my folds, he massaged my foot, and I felt like I was floating—my eyes in the back of my head, my breathing calm, my body relaxed. Except for the tingling that was coursing through my body. That was all the way live. Despite my effort to keep my mouth clean for the baby's sake, every curse word imaginable escaped my mouth as I felt myself about to climax, "Shit, Nico, fuck. Gahtdamn." He slowed, but then I told him, "No, don't stop." Just as he picked up the motion of his tongue, my body began to tense. "Right there," I yelled. Then there was a knock at the door, but thankfully, he didn't stop. Not until I was done, my head resting on the pillow.

Nico stood from the side of the bed and left the room. When he returned, he told me, "You gotta eat. Need some energy for what's next." He leaned over the bed and asked, "Do you have a robe I can grab for you?" His hand rubbed against my thigh. "Or you can sit out there naked, I'd prefer that anyway."

I pointed to my closet. "There's one beside the door."

He brought it back and reached for my hand, helping me place it on before tying it in the front. "Alright, let's eat." His arm was out for me to hold onto, and we walked into the dining room where he had set the containers on the table.

As if he hadn't just eaten my pussy for an appetizer, we sat across from each other and had a normal conversation. He asked, "When you do buy a house, what kind of house would you like?"

The house I grew up in was perfect, for me and my mom. Not too big, but enough room for us to each have our own space. That was what I considered when I replied, "Something comfortable, contemporary." I considered the baby who was kicking along with my voice. "A yard big enough for them to play in."

Nico was nodding his head along with me. "Nova lives in a nice neighborhood. Maybe I can take you over to visit one day."

I knew that Nova ran a successful tech startup, and his business was doing well. That was my reference when I told him, "I'm not sure I have the chops to be neighbors with Nova."

"Hmm." He shrugged. "Won't hurt to look."

I narrowed my eyes. "I suppose." Then I asked, "What about you? Have you considered leaving your apartment?"

He answered, "Maybe," before placing his fork down and eyeing my plate. "Had enough?" I had only eaten half my plate, but the way he was looking at me like he wanted to consume me had me craving him more than the lasagna.

"For now," I told him. And just like that, he was up from his seat and helping me out of mine.

In my room, he waited until I was on the bed again before he stripped out of his clothes like he was working a stage. Slowly lifting his shirt, revealing his washboard abs. Then unbuckling his pants and shimmying them down before standing there in his boxer briefs, his dick imprint on full display. He stared me down as his lip went between his teeth, his thumb hooked under the waist of his boxers, and then he let his dick free. I felt between my legs, the moisture making me think my water could have broken.

Nico leaned down and grabbed a condom, making a dramatic show of rolling it on over his dick. "Not like this worked before." He smacked his lips, and I laughed.

He reached his hand out for me, pulling me to the edge of the bed. He untied my robe, throwing off the sides from my shoulders. Then he unhooked my bra and kissed each of my nipples while I sucked in a breath. "You okay?" he asked, looking up at me.

"A little sensitive." I told him, and he moved his mouth to my neck, sucking there instead. I felt his hand between my legs, and I moaned as his fingers caressed. "Damn, Nico."

He turned me around, leaned me against the bed, and spread my legs. "Tell me if this gets uncomfortable." His voice was deep, reliant, but I didn't respond. I just braced myself against the bed, ready for what was coming next.

Each inch spread me wider, each thrust had me gripping the sheets, each kiss to the back of my neck had me about to lose it all. To think I was about to deny my body that level of pleasure. *For what?*

He fucked me thoroughly, painstakingly slow. He was as cautious with my body while he fucked me as he was when he carried me. And I appreciated it all, so much so that it was me who came first. He wasn't too far behind me, though, and when he finished, he pulled out and left the room again. I laid on the bed, too spent to move anywhere else.

"Let me," he whispered as he put a warm towel between my legs. "Do you need anything else?" he asked before he moved around again.

"Are you leaving?" I asked, the tears threatening to fall from my eyes, and I couldn't understand why.

"No," then he added, "Unless you want me to."

"No." I made room for him in the bed, and he laid behind me, my back curled into him, his arm wrapped around my belly.

"By the way," he told me, "I sold the bike."

I turned over my shoulder and searched his eyes. "You did?" He nodded his head with a slight smile on his face. "What are you driving now?"

"A Camaro."

"Still fast," I teased.

"But room for a car seat," he admitted.

Chapter Twenty-One

Nico

Basketball was my first love, but I enjoyed interviewing football players too. College football was as busy of a season for us at *All Around* as basketball season. Balancing the show schedule and my time with Destiny was becoming a challenge. I was determined to show her that I was committed though. When she reminded me about her thirty-week appointment, I asked, "Can I tag along?" because I had yet to be at one of her appointments. We talked about me being in the delivery room, and the thought of it all had me scared shitless. But going to her doctor's appointment felt like the way to ease some of that fear.

With us both working in the SportsOne building, we were able to carpool to the appointment in the middle of the day. I had even shared with my crew that I was with Destiny, and she was having my baby. It felt a little like a sitcom of some sort when it all came out, but they were happy for me still the same. George even told me, "Let me know when the shower is so I can send over a gift." Then when he asked, "You having a little Nico?"

I shook my head. "Actually, she hasn't found out yet." Then I corrected, "We haven't found out yet."

He tapped my shoulder. "For your sake, I hope it's a boy." He laughed, reminding me that, "Those girls will have you in a chokehold at birth." George had two little girls of his own.

"Don't freak the man out." That was my producer standing beside us when she told him, "Girls aren't *that* bad."

"I'm trying to tell you, man," George said with a serious face.

Those were the words that were on my mind as I waited in the lobby for Destiny. When I finally saw her I asked, "Do you think we can find out the sex of the baby today?"

The look on her face told me otherwise, but she asked, "Would it matter one way or the other?"

"I mean," I tried to tell her there were things to buy for a boy or a girl. "Right? Don't you want to have clothes and all that?" But really, I just wanted to know if I had a little basketball player in her belly. Then that's when everything came crashing down— the thought of a little boy, or a little girl, inheriting not only my basketball skills, but my heart condition.

We were walking, she was talking, but I didn't hear anything she said until she shouted, "Nico, the door." Right before I ran into it. She gasped, "Are you okay?"

I rubbed a hand across my forehead and laughed. Looking down at her I said, "I don't think that shit has ever happened to me."

Her eyes were wide when she asked again, "Are you okay?"

I nodded, "Yeah," but I didn't tell her what was on my mind. We continued walking, her talking, and me thinking. The entire ride to the doctor's office I spent thinking of a way to ask the doctor about the odds of the baby inheriting my condition. I knew my mom had passed it on to me, but I was hoping that's where the sharing would end.

When we pulled up to the office, I noted, "As long as I'm not getting pricked," she looked at me with a crooked smile, "I should survive this."

"Is that why your ass ran into an entire door?" We were walking through the door as she said it. "Because if the sight of blood makes you that scared, then the delivery room may be a no for you."

I shook my head. "I just won't look down." She cocked her head. "I don't think I need to see all that anyway." My eyes were wide as she left me to check in with the receptionist.

The waiting room wasn't packed. A few women had men tagging along, and others were sitting alone. "I should have been coming to these appointments with you," I noted, looking down at her beside me.

She brushed it off. "Most of them are not that exciting." I looked across the room at another man sitting beside his partner and wondered how many appointments he missed. "First I'll have to pee in a cup," she explained. "They'll check it for protein."

"In your pee?" I asked, not knowing why they'd need to do all that. Then she explained her levels had been high when she was in the hospital and that could have been a sign of pre-eclampsia. "Oh," was all I could say.

"After that I'll go to the room, a few checks of me, then the baby, then we are on our way."

I was thinking that was a good time to talk to her about my condition. As soon as I started with, "I have a question for the doctor," the nurse was calling her name. "Should I come with you now?" She nodded and I walked behind her. In the last couple of weeks alone, her walk had slowed and reminded me of a duck's waddle.

The doctor's office had that familiar smell that mine had, that extra sterile coldness that wasn't welcoming in the least. I sat in the room waiting for Destiny to finish filling her cup. The posters on the wall were different than the one's in my doctor's office. I didn't see the full anatomy, or even the advertisements for an annual check-up. I saw a woman's organs, blown up to proportions that had me intrigued. I was staring at the ovaries when Destiny walked in. "A lot happens down there, right?" I looked up to her. "The woman's body, it's amazing."

I nodded, especially when my gaze moved from the woman's organs to the womb. A picture of a baby curled up inside. "Now that right there is crazy." I pointed.

"Even more so when you can feel all that inside." Her hand rested on her stomach. Then she told me, "I need to get this gown on."

I looked around then asked, "Want my help?" The room was crowded, hardly leaving me room to give her privacy, although I'd seen all her body more than enough.

"I think I'm good." I watched as she peeled out of her shirt, pulled down the slacks that had a little pouch built in for her stomach, then off went her panties. If it weren't for her belly hanging over, I would have caught a glimpse of her pussy. She looked at me and said, "I don't even know what it looks like down there anymore," with a chuckle. She pulled on the gown, then a knock came at the door. "Come in," Destiny said.

A doctor and nurse came in and addressed Destiny first before noticing me beside the bed. "Oh, hi there." The doctor reached her hand out and introduced herself, "I'm Dr. Jackson."

"Hello, Dr. Jackson," I said, outstretching my hand to the Black woman who had a full smile on her face.

"Let's see how you are doing." The nurse started taking Destiny's blood pressure while the doctor started feeling around Destiny's stomach. "Have you been moving around okay?" I wanted to interject and let her know she was full-on waddling, but I figured that was a given.

Then she pulled out a machine, squirted some lube over Destiny's belly, and said, "Now the baby's turn." As she moved the wand around she noted, "And you don't know the sex yet, right?" Destiny nodded her head and I looked over at her.

"But if we can find out today that'd be great." I smiled and my heartbeat picked up. Destiny winked at me.

"Okay, if the baby cooperates." Dr. Jackson called out numbers and terms I wasn't familiar with to the nurse before saying, "If we'll know anything, it'll be now." She moved the wand and I watched the screen on the wall intently. Not able to recognize a penis or a vagina, I waited for her to speak. "It's a boy."

The gasp that escaped my mouth was audible to everyone in the room. The doctor looked over her shoulder and said, "I'd say you are happy to hear that, but honestly, I think you would have gasped either way." She laughed. "Everything is looking good," she addressed Destiny.

"Dr. Jackson," I interjected, "I have a heart condition, hypertrophic cardiomyopathy," the term leaving my mouth easily. "I know it's genetic."

Before I could continue, Dr. Jackson responded, "Unfortunately, that'll be something we'll test for after the baby is born." I nodded my head, feeling less relieved. "Now Destiny..." She then went on to tell her about the next appointment.

After Destiny was dressed and checked out with the receptionist, we were walking back to the car when I asked, "Have time for lunch?"

She looked at me, her face somber when she responded, "I think that's a good idea." Neither of us said much on the ride across town, where I pulled up to the café near SportsOne. When we were seated across from each other Destiny asked, "That's what was on your mind? Earlier?" I nodded my head.

Her lip curled up. "The thought never even crossed my mind. Thank you for asking." Then she looked down.

I reached across the table to grab her hand. "Don't let it worry you, okay?"

She wagged her head and told me, "Easier said than done, unfortunately." Then she stood from the table. "Let me use the bathroom then we can probably head back before I'm too tired to go back to work." She laughed.

I watched her make her way down the hall of the café. My eyes were on the food on our table when I heard her voice, away from the table. I looked up and saw a man standing beside her. The conversation didn't seem friendly, and her head was shaking, back and forth.

It didn't take me long to cross the restaurant, standing behind her, "What's going on?" I asked more to her than the man standing beside her.

She looked at me. "Nico, this is," she pointed to him, "my ex."

Before she could recite the introduction of him, his mouth was falling open. "This your man?" he asked.

"I am," I stated confidently, and noticed Destiny looked between the both of us. "You good, bruh?"

"Yeah, I'm good. Great actually." He snickered. "Glad I missed the bullet on that one." Then he cocked his head to the side. "It's yours, right?"

"Jensen, I just told you it was his baby. What's your problem?"

Then his face grew cold when he said, "No problem at all, just pretty convenient for you to have a whole man, and what looks like a baby that's about to drop any day now. Considering we broke up *this year.*"

She was shaking her head, and I decided whatever it was Jensen was on, she didn't need it. "Sounds like you are upset that I found value where you found none. We are good over here." I grabbed Destiny's hand and led us to our table, picked up her purse, then walked us out of the restaurant. Outside, I looked at her and asked, "Are you okay?"

"Today's just been a lot." She sighed, "I don't think I'll be any good at work."

I felt her on that. "Send your manager a note, I'm taking us home."

Chapter Twenty-Two

Destiny

Everything was going good. Great, even. Except for the reminder from Nico about his heart condition, and the fact that my baby could have inherited it. Then there was the run-in with Jensen, and that was fucking bananas. But me and the baby, we were doing good. I was walking into thirty-two weeks of pregnancy feeling like everything was going to work out.

I had baby showers planned and an apartment full of baby stuff Monroe helped me pick out. Okay, there was also that, I was still staying in a one-bedroom apartment. But that was fine, it would be fine. I tried to convince myself as I sat on the couch looking at the space that already felt smaller with the amount of baby stuff laying around.

The phone rang, and Nico's name popped up. I answered with a smile on my face until I heard his voice. "Destiny," he said, sounding downright dreadful. "Busy?"

If I wasn't at work, I was sitting on the couch, and most of the time he was sitting around with me. I reminded him anyway, "The way my energy is set up, the thought of being busy is too tiring." I laughed, but he didn't even seem to crack a smile. "Sheesh, you okay?" I asked.

He hesitated, and I knew something was wrong. The phone was pressed against my ear as I waited for him to respond. "I saw this man today," he started to describe him, "Looked to be a few years older than me." Where he was going had me confused. "He had one of those baby backpacks on."

"Baby backpack?" I repeated. Then thought about it, "You mean a carrier?"

"Yeah," he said with little enthusiasm, "That thing. I watched him walk across the lobby of the apartment. Then as he made his way outside to the parking garage. Baby strapped in, diaper bag on his shoulder." Then he waited a minute before he said, "And you know what was happening the entire time?"

"No, what?" I was invested in the story, but more so, wondering why he was so intrigued by an everyday occurrence.

"The baby was crying," he said as if it was a huge revelation.

I let him know, "I hear they do that often." But it was like he was deflated. "Nico, what's going on?"

"What if I can't do that? What if whatever it is that should trigger a parent to kick into action after the baby is born doesn't happen with me?"

"God forbid, it didn't trigger for either of us," I joked, but Nico was far from laughing. "Wait, you are really worried, aren't you?"

"Ever wonder why you have such a strong diversion to certain things? Like you were born not liking milk only to find out you are deathly allergic to it."

His thoughts were all over the place, and I wasn't exactly following. The one thing I could tell was that he was terrified. "Are you saying that you never wanted kids, and that may be because you'll be a terrible father?" My face had twisted up, and I shifted a couple of times on the couch as the baby found his favorite spot under a rib.

Nico simply replied, "Yeah."

"Or maybe," I argued, "You just never know you want something you think is unattainable. You hadn't been in a relationship before so maybe the idea of kids was too foreign to you, at the time." Then I considered, "Are you having second thoughts about all of this?" He was quiet, I could only hear him breathing softly. "Nico, you have eight weeks to figure this shit out, but I can't be worried about it right now."

"Destiny, wait," he pleaded.

"No, Nico, you are feeling some type of way about all of this. You need to work it out. But I can't be worried about the baby coming and you ghosting the both of us when you realize shit is real. Because you know what," I had leaned forward, "I don't have the luxury of walking away. It's me and this baby for the rest of my life." I hung up the phone before he could say anything else.

My phone sat beside me, and I tried to calm my nerves. My hands were shaking and the tears, the ones that had no problem falling, were trekking down my face.

"I can't believe this shit," I shouted then covered my mouth and whispered, "Sorry, little man," with a gentle caress to my belly.

The pile of baby clothes and diapers were in a corner, and I thought of the person who would let me vent without judgment. "He said what?" was the first thing Monroe said after I told her all about the conversation with Nico.

"I don't have the energy to deal with his self-doubt, or indecisiveness." I told her, "Eight weeks to go, and I just need to get to the finish line. You know?"

"Okay, in his defense—" she started.

But I barked, "His defense? As if he could have one?"

"Listen, have you not second guessed all of this at some point?" I thought about the day she and I were in the baby store and the thought of feeding the baby in the middle of the night startled me. I even asked her what if I didn't wake up when the baby needed me. I had freaked the fuck out. "He probably should have discussed it with someone else, maybe, but at least he trusted he could be vulnerable with you."

"Vulnerable?" I repeated. "That's one thing, but straight up sounding like he was about to hide out, skirt his responsibilities is an entirely different thing."

With a calm voice, she told me, "Is that what he said though?" Her voice hitching. "Because what you just told me sounds like he's scared, sharing his thoughts, but he didn't exactly say, 'Destiny, I don't want to be in my child's life.'"

"Okay, maybe that was my emotions kicking in." My hands settled, and I felt at ease again. "I was a little harsh. I should call him."

She quickly shouted, "No, you shouldn't. You were probably harsh, but," her emphasis was lingering, "give him some time to think it over, let him come back around."

It had been seven days without a single word from Nico. We didn't run into each other at work, and he didn't call. His midweek visits didn't happen either. By Saturday, I had gone full circle with my emotions, and by the time I was walking into the baby shower my mom was hosting I was disguising the anger I had built up toward him.

Everyone knew that we, or that I was expecting a baby boy. So, the royal blue dress I decided on wasn't ruining the surprise for anyone. Inside, the flowers, balloons, diaper towers, and desserts were beautiful, and all dripping in blue. My mom found me near the dessert table, sneaking a brownie, when she asked, "How does it look?"

With the brownie at the tip of my mouth, I looked around and told her, "It's beautiful, thank you."

"Glad I vetoed the basketball idea." Her nose scrunched up. "Especially now." When I shared that Nico wouldn't be making an appearance, my mom had a less than savory response. "No need for us to dwell on that though."

"Mom," I said after taking a bite of the brownie. "Not now, okay?"

She waved her hand in the air. "Don't worry about me, I won't even mention his name again." She rubbed my belly then disappeared to the other side of the room, where she greeted everyone walking in with arms full of gifts.

Despite knowing that Nico wasn't going to show up, it didn't stop me from checking the front door each time someone walked in. The dirty diaper, candy bar game, had me thinking about him and all the times we bantered about who would be on diaper duty.

"Time to open gifts," Monroe announced. "You, Mama, should sit right here."

I was sitting in the queen's chair, in front of a room full of women who were there to celebrate me. All of it was overwhelming, especially when I realized the one person I wanted to share that time with most was nowhere in sight.

There were onesies, pajamas, books, bottles, diapers—tons of diapers. Then there was a gift Monroe saved for last. Telling me, "I don't know what this one is, but I love the wrapping." Then she bent down and handed me the card that was attached. Nico's name scribbled on the front. I looked at Monroe and she just placed a hand on my shoulder.

I held the card close but decided to open the gift first. Inside was a brown bear, with a jersey, and on the back the name "Maxwell." I looked up at Monroe again, and she smiled. My guests were all dispersing as my mom instructed everyone to grab dessert.

The card rested between my two hands and when I pulled it out I read, "Baby Nico, I want this to be a reminder that we will always be connected. And if you start to miss me, listen to the heartbeat. Love, Daddy." By the time I finished reading the card the tears weren't only flowing but so was the snot. I sniffled and looked to Monroe. Before I could ask, she was already handing me a tissue. "Thank you."

"Why are you crying?" I looked to the other side of me where my mother stood. "What happened?"

I sighed, "The bear is from Nico."

She groaned. "And here you are crying when you should be celebrating." She frowned, crossed her arms across her chest and everything. I felt her lean in close, blotting my face with another tissue. "Now, get yourself together and eat a piece of your beautiful cake." Then she bragged, "It tastes as good as it looks." She looked at Monroe. "C'mon, Monroe, you too."

The teddy bear was still clutched in my hands, and in that moment, it was me who was missing Nico. I stopped walking across the room and raised the bear to my ear, pressed its chest, and listened to the heartbeat.

Monroe placed a hand on my back and told me, "You are going to be okay, girl."

I nodded my head because I knew, no matter what, I would be okay. "With him," I paused, "Or without him. I'm good."

Chapter Twenty-Three

Nico

Catching feelings had me all twisted inside, and I was glad when the producer told me *All Around* was on the road again. Flights would have to do it for me. My suitcase was open on the floor, stretched out, when I heard a knock on my door. I wasn't expecting anyone, and when I saw the woman standing on the other side through the peep hole, my face twisted up.

"Ms. Harlow," I announced as I opened the door. "Everything okay?" I stepped out of the doorway and welcomed her inside.

She walked in carefully. "I hope I'm not interrupting."

"I was," I pointed to my room, "Just packing."

She moved further into my apartment. "Oh, going somewhere?" I felt like she was judging me in the way her eyes were scanning my space, especially since she had been there before. She had seen most of my apartment during the time Destiny stayed with me.

"I'm on the road for the show," I told her. Curious about her visit, I tried another approach. "Ms. Harlow, was there something you needed?"

She ran her hand across my kitchen counter. "Nico." I fixed my stance as I waited for her to speak. "Destiny might not share much about her father. He decided when she was five he not only wanted to be out of my life," she was frowning and her face reminded me of Destiny, "he also wanted nothing else to do with Destiny."

"I understand he wasn't in her life." My lips grew tight as I waited for her to explain whatever else it was she needed me to know.

"I raised Destiny by myself." She held her head up straight. "And I did a damn good job."

I nodded my head because Destiny was amazing. "I agree, Ms. Harlow."

She held up a finger. "If you are second guessing being in their life, they'll be better off if you decide to walk away now. Don't let her think you will be there, then leave. Don't let that baby get to know you, and then you disappear. They don't need that. They'd be better off not having you at all."

I cocked my head, and my mouth opened then shut. Half of me wanted to argue that I would never leave them. Then the other half of me doubted my ability to be there for Destiny or the baby. I uttered, "I understand." I walked to the door and asked, "Was there anything else you wanted to share?"

She shook her head then looked at the frame sitting on the counter. "He's going to be loved no matter what."

"He will be loved," I said of baby Maxwell, whose ultrasound picture she was staring at.

She sucked her teeth before walking to the door. I opened it and let her out. "Be safe, Ms. Harlow," I said to her back.

A few hours later, I was landing in Mississippi. The *All Around* team was ready to interview the top football recruit—the one who could have played at any college in the country and decided to play for an HBCU.

The visit from Ms. Harlow had me off my game, up until the moment I stepped foot on the college campus. "Dion's doing the damn thing on this campus, right?" I looked at Jermaine, who was walking beside me.

"Yeah." His face didn't look as enthused as mine did though. "Except it's just the athletics side of things." He pointed in the opposite direction. "Did you see what we drove through to get over here?" His nose crinkled. "I don't know what you plan on asking Trey, but make sure you ask him how he feels about this school not having the same resources as the schools who recruited him."

I laughed. "And remind him of what he could have had?"

"Hmm." He shook his head. "Guess making him regret his choice wouldn't be the best look, huh?"

"Understatement of the year." I laughed. The noise of the band practicing nearby had the ground rumbling. "But he also wouldn't have had that at any other school," I noted. We walked into the training facility and were greeted by an assistant coach, Trevor.

"We are happy to have you here. Trey's a fantastic athlete." Then his voice dropped. "And he's surrounded by an amazing team. If you have time, I don't think we'd mind if you spoke with others as well." He grinned, and I knew what he wanted us to do. Bring even more attention to the team than just the star recruit.

I understood and told Jermaine, "We'll try to work that in, okay?" Jermaine nodded his head.

"Great." Trevor continued walking through the facility. "And most people have seen this on SportsOne, but if you want to capture any footage of the facility, feel free." He directed that at Jermaine.

Then he finally stepped in front of a few players and called out, "Trey," as a young guy stepped forward. As a corner back, he wasn't the biggest guy in the locker room, but he was still a couple of inches taller than me. His hand reached out before any of us could say anything.

"Trey," I said, shaking his hand, "thank you for taking the time to talk to us." I told him, "I know this week is busy with homecoming, and being your first I'm sure you are excited." His grin grew wide.

"One of the reasons I landed here at Jackson State," he told us before Jermaine even had his camera up. "I visited last year during the homecoming game, and let's just say, hands down, that experience did it for me."

Being that I, too, had gone to an HBCU, I could relate. "I'm sure it did." I looked at Jermaine setting up his equipment. "We'll give Jermaine time before we start." I looked for Trevor and asked, "Is this the best place for us to record?" The lighting wasn't the best, but Jermaine could make do with that. "Should we have something with the mascot or school name in the background?"

He pointed up the hallway. "Yes, we have a spot over here. With the tiger." We all moved toward the tiger, and as we did, I explained to Trey that the questions would be straight forward, the film would be edited, and if there was anything we needed to cut at the end we would do that.

"I'm good," he smiled and reminded me, "I've done a few of these."

"Right." I laughed and wiped my hand across my mouth. "With other networks."

Jermaine tapped in. "I'm ready when you are, Nico."

I straightened my shoulders, looked at Trey, and said, "Trey, this year's number one recruit. The decision you made to join Jackson State stunned the sports world." I looked to him. "You had a number of Division One schools who were interested in you." He was nodding his head. "As you stand here preparing to get ready for the homecoming game, which for those who don't know, at an HBCU it's the biggest game of the season, do you have any regrets?"

He wagged his head, and I could see Jermaine's eyes narrowing from behind the camera. "On that field," his glance was beyond me, "with this team," he looked the other direction toward the players in the locker room, "I have none." I was about to ask my next question when he added, "But there's one thing I regret." He cleared his throat and made eye contact with the camera. "I wish my dad was here to see it."

As a sports journalist, it was my job to know the background of the athlete I was interviewing. For Trey, I knew his dad passed away in Trey's junior year of high school. In response to his regret, I told him, "I am sure your father would be so proud of you." Then I shared, "Not only for what you are doing on the field, but for the decision you made. You will make a difference for the sport, for other Black athletes, and certainly for this school."

The interview wrapped up after a few more questions and as Jermaine packed up the camera, he looked at me and asked, "Thought we weren't going to talk about regrets?"

"What can I say, it was fresh on my mind." I shrugged. "I guess." He laughed, but Trey's response had me thinking more about the baby, and what life would be like for him if I didn't show up.

Jermaine wasn't the first person on my "call a friend," card, but he was there, so I asked, "Hey, have you ever thought about kids?"

He looked at me as he loaded his camera into the trunk of the rental. We had to make our way across campus to catch footage of the pep rally. "In this job, seems like thinking about kids is a given." He smirked.

"No," I shook my head, "have you thought about having them?"

He slammed the trunk and pointed to me, "Of course, man." He slapped my shoulder. "I'll be like you one day, a little baby on the way. You ready?" He climbed into the driver's seat.

I buckled up on the passenger side and took my time before I replied, "No, not ready at all."

He looked over his shoulder as he put the car in reverse. "I don't think anyone is ever ready." Then he said, "But I'm sure just like everyone else who isn't ready, you'll be good." We were headed across campus, and he blurted, "I bet these homecoming parties are about to be wild, man."

I nodded my head. "I bet they are."

"You wouldn't be up for any of that, though, would you?"

I couldn't believe the words that came out of my mouth when I said, "No, I should probably get to the room when I finish up."

Chapter Twenty-Four

Destiny

My apartment still looked like a mess, despite all the arranging and re-arranging I was doing. Having a second person in the house, even though they would be the size of my arm, added much more stuff. Stuff I couldn't find a place for. My mama told me I was nesting, but if nesting was meant to get the house ready before the baby arrived—I wasn't feeling very accomplished.

With only a few days left before the due date, I felt extremely unprepared. I had stopped holding my breath to hear from Nico and made a back-up plan for the delivery room. It would be my mom and Monroe in the room with me.

As I moved around a few baskets of clothes, the teddy bear Nico bought for the baby, who remained nameless, fell out. I held it in my arms and sniffed, although there was no scent of him there. I looked at the jersey, and his surname on the back brought a slight smile to my face, and the baby kicked my side. I rubbed my belly and whispered, "Watch it, those hurt now."

I pressed the bear's chest and pulled it to my ear to listen to the heartbeat, and as I did there was another sharp pain in my belly. They had been coming more often, but the birthing class I took reminded me to breathe through them, and that's what I did as I moved to the couch with the teddy bear in my hand.

My phone was on the coffee table, and as I looked between it and the teddy bear, I decided instead of waiting on Nico to call me, I would call him. So, I did. He answered on the first ring, "Destiny? You okay," he asked.

I had been fairly calm with him over the course of the pregnancy, but something about the way he asked that brought out another side of me. "Okay? Oh, I'm just over here about to birth your baby out of my vagina in a couple of days. Haven't heard from you in weeks, but yeah, I'm good. How are you?"

"Whoa," was all he said.

"Nico, what the fuck?" I finally asked. "You know what, I don't know why I called. Now that I have you, though, I just want to know, are you in or are you out?" Before he could respond, another pain came across my belly, and I breathed a little harder.

"Destiny, you are breathing hard, what's going on?"

When the pain passed, I told him, "That's been happening, and will likely happen more as I get closer," I reminded him.

"Destiny, I need to apologize. I didn't handle this right." As he spoke, I breathed, waiting for the pain to subside again. "When your mom told me you could do it alone, I started to think that was best."

"What?" I breathed a little harder. "What are you even talking about right now, Nico?" I managed to say between breaths.

"Your mom, she came to my place and explained the situation with your dad. Told me that it would be less painful for me to leave the two of you alone now, instead of leaving you later."

I tried to comprehend what he was saying, but the baby was having soccer practice in my stomach. "She said that?" Nothing of that was repeated to me. I didn't even know she had gone to visit him. Not even after I complained that he had ghosted me. "When did she say that?"

"It was last month, before I went to Jackson State, actually." I knew exactly when that was because our team worked on the marketing for that interview. The campaign results were remarkable. "But that's neither here nor there, I'm my own man. I should have done what I felt was right all along. Stopped doubting myself." My belly tensed again. "I may not earn the world's greatest father award, but I want to try, to be the dad our son can be proud of." Then he whispered, "With no regret." That made me think of his interview at Jackson State.

"Tell me something, Nico," I paused as the pain subsided, "was it the interview with Trey? Is that what made you come full circle, again?"

"Destiny, my thoughts have been all over the place. I will admit that. The interview with Trey definitely gave me the kick in the ass I needed to get my shit together."

Then I dared to ask, "And us?"

He laughed. "That's the only thing I was sure about it in this entire situation." Instead of feeling all warm and fuzzy inside, another pain shot through my stomach, and as I breathed, Nico told me, "I only know what I've seen in movies, but Destiny, are you in labor right now?"

Through gritted teeth, I told him, "You should have been at my birthing classes."

"I'm on my way to get you." Then he warned, "Don't talk, but stay on the phone." I placed the phone beside me and rested my head back as another pain came pounding through. As I sat there, rubbing my belly and my back, I could hear air rushing past the phone.

By the time he knocked at the door, I was breathing a little harder, pains were coming quicker. I managed to make it to the door and shouted, "My bag, can you grab my bag?" Nico ran into the apartment, frantically looking everywhere. "My room," I shouted.

Then we were off. Thank God for his Camaro because we got to the hospital in record time. He pulled in front of the emergency entrance, and a nurse greeted me with a wheelchair after he ran inside. "I'll meet you in there," was the last thing I heard from Nico as the nurse wheeled me to a room.

I went straight to the maternity floor, and when I saw Nico again, I instructed him to call my mom and Monroe. The nurse took one look at me and said, "I hope they are nearby."

Nico stuttered when he asked, "The baby is coming, today?"

"The doctor can confirm, but I'm pretty sure the baby will be here in the next couple of hours, if not sooner."

"Oh." He started pacing the floor with my phone in his hand. "Okay, I'll call them now."

There were machines, nurses, a doctor, and Nico pacing the floor as we waited for the doctor to tell us, "Okay, you are at eight centimeters, when you get to ten, you'll start to push."

I heard my mom's voice, and tears started streaming down my face. "I'm here, I'm here," she shouted as she made her way to my bedside. The nurses were prepping around us, and my mom looked up to Nico and stated, "Nico, I've got it from here." With a stern look, she told him, "You can leave."

He looked to her, then to me with his eyes narrowed and walked out of the room.

"Mom, what are you doing?"

She rubbed a hand through my hair. "Destiny, it's fine, we got this."

I shook my head and told her, "Stop, just stop." Her hand stopped rubbing, and I said, "No, stop trying to push him away." I wanted to say more but my stomach tensed again. I tried to breathe through it, tried to close my eyes, but the pain became unbearable and I screamed.

I heard a nurse shout, "It may be time," before she moved between my legs.

"Ms. Harlow." My eyes were still closed, but I heard Nico's voice. "I have to be here. I want to be here for Destiny and the baby." Then on the other side of me, I felt his hand on top of mine. "Destiny, is that okay?"

"Yes," I mumbled as I felt my belly beginning to tense again. The nurse announced she was getting the doctor and it was time to push.

The plan was to have Monroe and my mom in the room with me, but Monroe wasn't there. I looked to Nico and told him, "You stay right here," then I looked to my mama and said, "Can you keep an eye out down there?"

"Of course," she said through a tight grin.

The doctor walked in, and as he went between my legs, I tried to remember the instructions from my birthing class. *Push like you have to shit*, was the only thing I could remember when the doctor told me, "On your next contraction, I want you to take a deep breath, and push."

I looked up to Nico and shook my head. "I'm not ready."

He wiped a hand across my forehead and said, "You are ready. We are ready. And you got this." He looked toward the doctor then back to me and tried to have a comforting smile, but he looked just as scared as I felt.

"And push," the doctor shouted as I was trying to navigate through the pain.

Ten pushes, and my mom promising, "You're almost there, Destiny, I can see his head," then the baby was out. I was relieved when his cries sang out. I had cried over my pregnancy, often, but nothing like the tears that came out when they laid the baby on my chest. "He's beautiful, honey." My mom looked down at him.

"Wow, look at him." Then I heard Nico sniffling and had to look up to witness it myself. "Damn, got me crying over here." He wiped a hand across his face and cleared his throat.

I heard another voice, as someone rushed into the room. "I did not miss it," Monroe shouted. "I can't believe I missed it." She joined me at the side of the bed, beside my mom. "And he's here. He didn't miss it? Oh, I'm glad." She pouted her lips and said, "Aw, my little baby, he's here."

"We just need to get him cleaned up." The nurse reached for him and I handed him over as I looked at Nico, who promised he would stay with him till they brought him back. "Thank you."

Monroe patted my head and said, "I should have known your ass was going to have a quick delivery. Always efficient," she joked.

"My ass almost didn't make it to the hospital." I looked at my mom then said, "Nico was the one who told me I needed to come." Monroe squinted. "We were on the phone, and the pains were coming quick." I gritted my teeth. "I thought it was Braxton Hicks."

She nodded her head. "Well, thankfully you didn't have my nephew on the floor."

My mom interjected, "Dear God, glad you didn't. I should have had you staying at the house this close to your due date."

"It's fine, all worked out." I looked over to Nico, who was

watching over the baby like a hawk. When the nurse was finished, she had him wrapped like a burrito, and I watched Nico's face as she handed him over. He didn't move, his hands were cautious as he held him. "You can bring him over here."

He looked over and said, "Yeah, right, I'll bring him over." But his feet didn't move.

The nurse placed an arm on his shoulder and said, "It's okay, just walk carefully, keep him tucked in close." Nico did just that and walked at a snail's pace as he made it back to me.

As I looked at our son, I thought, "Now the next thing is to name this beautiful baby." I looked between my mom, Monroe, then finally to Nico.

Monroe offered, "How about Nash?" She leaned in, looking at his face, then scrunched her nose. "I think it fits." I looked down at the baby—his tiny nose, round cheeks, and dark black hair.

"Nova, Nico, and Nash." I looked up to Nico and waited for him to respond.

He wagged his head, his eyes never leaving the baby's face. "I think I like it."

"Me too." But then it was time for my mom to add her two cents.

"I was thinking we honor your grandfather." My eyebrows raised. "Henry."

All of us repeated, "Henry?" I laughed afterward and shook my head. "He does not look like a Henry. We won't have my baby running around kindergarten getting bullied for his old name." My mom winced. "Sorry, Papa Henry was amazing, but..." I shook my head again. "I think Nash fits."

Whether Nico was there for the delivery or not—even if he decided he wouldn't be in our lives—I didn't want to ignore that he was half of the baby. As we were transferred to the room where we would stay for the next couple of days, Monroe and my mom left to grab dinner for us. But Nico never left. Not even when I insisted he should probably go home to grab clothes.

He told me, "I already texted Nova, he's bringing a bag for me."

I challenged, "Do you want to go home and take a shower?" He shook his head again.

"It looks like he's sleeping right now." My eyes were on Nash's resting face.

He reached for him and comfortably held him in his arms and told me, "Cool, go ahead and get some sleep." My eyes went wide as I watched him sit on the couch beside me. "It's okay, we'll be good right here." Then he assured me, "Besides, the nurse is helpful. If I need something I'll ask her."

I nodded slowly and let my eyes close gently.

Chapter Twenty-Five

Nico

I wasn't one to protest for justice, hadn't been a person who got overly involved in social issues. A few days before it was time to return to work after being off with Destiny and Nash for a couple of weeks, though, I was ready to march to the capital. Destiny had three months of maternity leave. I had two weeks. Two weeks to help her as much as possible, whenever possible. I wasn't ready to leave them though.

While camping out at Destiny's apartment, although it was small, we were able to get into somewhat of a routine. She fed him when he woke up, I changed his diapers and coaxed him back to sleep—then repeat.

I thought it was working pretty well, I didn't really want to disrupt it, but I knew I had to get back to work. *All Around* had been flexible over the pregnancy, allowing me to stay in Atlanta for interviews and work from home when I wasn't on air. But my producer warned me it was time to get back to business, in the office.

Nash was as sweet a baby as any I had been around. That wasn't saying much considering I hadn't been around too many babies though. So far, changing diapers and rocking him was pretty easy. For some reason, though, Destiny didn't seem to have the same sentiment. I was standing over the couch changing Nash's diaper when I saw her stomp through the living room into the kitchen. I asked, "Destiny, what's going on?" She hadn't seemed like herself since she came home from the hospital.

Before we left, the doctor warned that she needed to get as much sleep as possible, eat, and stay hydrated to avoid postpartum depression. But instead of resting when Nash was sleep, she insisted on doing random cleaning or folding laundry. Even though I was there helping with that too.

"All this stuff," she pointed, "It's just so much." Then she burst into tears. She cried a lot while she was pregnant, but nothing compared to how much she cried since we had been home.

"What can I do?" I asked as I snapped Nash's onesie.

"Nothing. Unless you can magically double the space we have here." I picked up Nash and walked toward her. "And what else is going on?" I looked at her swipe tears from her eyes.

"How am I going to do this when you're back at work?" I reminded her that her mom was taking time off to be there with her. "And she'll do nothing but tell me how I'm doing things wrong." She groaned. "I don't see that making anything better."

Nash had fallen asleep in my arms. I moved him to the bassinet then snuck up behind Destiny, kissing her neck. Her hair was all over her head, and she may or may not have had the same outfit on for a couple of days—but I didn't care. I wrapped my arms around her waist, and she flinched in my arms. "You okay?"

"Nico," she sighed. I kissed the other side of her neck. "Six weeks," she said bluntly, reminding me that her lady parts were still fresh from delivery.

"I know." I informed her, "No fucking for another month, but," I turned her around in my arms, "kissing doesn't count, right?" I laid my lips on hers, but she pulled away.

With her hand on my chest, she shoved me away then said, "I'm just not ready for that, yet." She explained as she wiped her hand across her hair, "I don't feel like myself."

"I get it." I opened my arms wide and she walked into my embrace. "I still think you are beautiful, and this body did what it needed to do to get Nash here." I let my hand rub against her shrinking belly.

"Yeah, yeah," she mumbled. Then I heard her sniffling. I looked down to see a fresh stream of tears rolling down her face.

"We have maybe one hour before he's up again. How about I fill the tub for you?" She wiped her face and nodded.

I left her in the kitchen, started the stream of water, and filled it with bubbles. When it was ready, I walked back to the kitchen but found Destiny on the couch sleeping. I pulled a blanket from the other side of the couch and laid it over her.

With my phone I quietly made my way into the kitchen, the only space in the apartment without someone sleeping peacefully, and called Ms. Harlow. She was the only person I thought could help Destiny, but the last person I wanted to talk to. She liked me less than before, if that was at all possible.

"Nico?" she asked when she answered.

"Ms. Harlow, do you have a minute?" It was after hours, and I suspected she was home from work.

"Is this about Button?" She gave him the nickname in the hospital and refused calling him Nash, ever. When I told her it was about Destiny, she paused before repeating, "Destiny?"

"Yes, I am worried she hasn't been acting like herself since coming home."

She rushed to a conclusion, telling me, "I'm sure when you are back at work and I'm there helping her, she'll start feeling better." I tried not to laugh at that because I knew Destiny didn't have the same thought about her helping out.

"Because she needs her mom or because you don't think she needs me?"

"The latter," she said dryly. "Not only does she have to worry about Button, but she's worried about pleasing you."

"Pleasing me?" I repeated a little too loudly, and I saw Destiny shift on the couch. Lowering my voice, I asked, "How exactly do you think she is pleasing me?"

"Hmph," she grunted, and I imagined a time where her mother and I would ever get along. It was looking like never. "Doing whatever you need to make sure you don't up and leave."

Ms. Harlow was an intelligent woman, or so I thought. But she was talking reckless, and not making any sense. "I was hoping you could suggest something that would help, but I'm not feeling you have any solutions other than me kicking rocks." I told her, "I'll let you go." Before she could say anything, I had hung up the phone.

I opened the cabinet and finished putting the dishes away. That was done, then I moved toward the living room to start folding the clothes, but the basket was only half finished when I heard Nash crying. Destiny woke up, rubbing her eyes. "I got him," I said, but she climbed off the couch and moved toward the bedroom.

"And feed him what?" She looked over her shoulder. "I'm the one he needs."

The next couple of days, nothing changed, except she

snapped more and there was nothing I could do or say that changed her mood.

It was the morning when I was returning to the office when her mom showed up bright and early, rocking a huge smile. She waved to me as I walked to the door. "No need to rush back." She had Nash cozied in her lap.

Not much had changed around the office, although I shouldn't have expected much because it was only *two weeks* since I had been gone. George was the first to greet me when I walked in. As we prepared for our segment he asked, "Alright, let us see them." I had the show's lineup in my hand, and I looked toward him.

"See what?"

He cocked his head to the side. "The baby." He laughed. "Pictures, of course."

My face grew into a smile, and I opened the album I had on my phone, collecting daily pictures of Nash. "Man, I have so many." I laughed. I started flipping and describing Nash's personality. Then I told him, "I don't even know what I would have done with a girl because of how he has me." I smirked.

"Are we looking at pictures of baby boy?" My producer walked in and looked over our shoulder. "He's adorable, Nico," she gushed. "Alright, makes what I'm about to tell you a little hard to say."

I closed the photos and stuffed my phone in my pocket. "What's up?"

She cringed before sharing, "I need you to get on the road." I knew that was coming, our road tours were doing well with our audience. I just didn't expect her to say, "This weekend."

I cleared my throat. "This weekend?" I looked over at George, who had avoided looking at me.

"Yeah, to cover a few unsuspected basketball players." She

mentioned, "There are a couple of teams who may end up in the championship game, who have never been there before. We'll need you on the road for a couple of weeks."

Although the thought was intriguing, the idea of leaving Destiny and Nash already wasn't exactly appealing. But I told her, "Okay."

"Great, we'll get your travel arrangements booked."

For the rest of the day I had to think how I'd tell Destiny I had to leave. I knew one thing was for sure, her mama couldn't be anywhere around when I told her.

When I made it back to her apartment that night, I asked, "Hey, Destiny, your mama still here?" She didn't have to answer because she came out of the bedroom, closing the door softly.

"Still here," she announced. She grabbed her purse, though, and told Destiny, "Now that he's here, I'll let him do his daddy duties." She leaned over Destiny on the couch and kissed her forehead. "I'll see you in the morning." As she walked past me, she just shook her head.

"Good night, Ms. Harlow." Destiny stood from the couch and walked over to me. "How was your day?" She started moving things around in the kitchen, although it was clean already.

"She told me that I hadn't been burping him well." Then she opened a cabinet and slammed a cup down. "Told me that I needed to be faster when giving him a bath." I walked up behind her and pulled her toward me, resting my chin on her head. "Nico," and I already knew what she was going to say.

Before she could finish, I told her, "I know, I just want you to relax a bit." I massaged her shoulders. "You are a good mom, Destiny." I felt bad that instead of telling her I could replace her mom, I had to leave town.

She turned to face me, her eyes sunken, eyelids swollen. "Thank you."

I nodded my head. "I need to tell you something." Her eyes narrowed. "I have to go out of town for two weeks."

"Already?" She rolled her eyes. "Of course, you do." She pushed away. "Guess I better get used to my mama telling me how bad of a mom I am." She went back to opening and closing cabinets.

The day I left for my first college on the tour, I kissed Nash on his forehead and held Destiny in my arms a little longer. Long enough for her mom to tell me, "Okay, already, you'll probably be late for your flight or something." She fanned her hand toward me. "Go."

"Bye, Ms. Harlow," I said as I walked to the front door. She was someone I would not miss, and did not miss. After five days on the road, in fact, I hadn't thought much about her. But Nash and Destiny, were a constant thought on my mind. They had me rushing back to my room to call and check on them at the end of each day.

Thursday night rolled around, and Jermaine insisted, "We should hit up happy hour." He tapped my shoulder. "Just a couple of drinks then you can go to your room and watch your kid's face till he falls asleep." He was laughing.

"Alright, just one drink," I told him as we walked through the hotel lobby.

"Just one." He shrugged his shoulders.

The hotel's bar was packed, the bar hardly had any open seats, and the tables were also full. "Might as well grab food too." The bartender walked over, and I ordered, "I'll take a basket of wings, and a Hennessey and Coke." Jermaine ordered a drink and food too.

While we were seated, Jermaine struck up a conversation with a couple of women sitting beside him. I hadn't paid them much attention, at first. But one of them moved between me and Jermaine. She asked, "What's your name?"

"I'm Nico, yours?"

"I'm Gina." She smiled. "Nice to meet you." She continued throwing questions to me, and I continued answering, not giving her much other than a one-or two-word response. "Are you two staying here at the hotel, or just here for happy hour?"

"We are staying at the hotel." I was tempted to ask her the same, just to keep the conversation flowing, but decided not to.

That didn't stop her from telling me, "Nice," with a wink, "we are both here for a conference." As she was saying, "Maybe we can," she leaned into my ear, and I looked beyond her to see Jermaine staring wide-eyed, "go up to your room, or mine."

I eased away from her mouth, ignoring her question. I looked to Jermaine and told him, "I think I'm going to go on up." Gina was collecting her purse from the counter, but I let her know, "I'm going up alone." I threw a couple of twenties on the bar and walked away.

Chapter Twenty-Six

Destiny

"It's just you and me, Nash," I whispered to him as he screamed at the top of his lungs. "Please, just take a nap." I had repeated that a few times through the night, and already a couple since the sun had been shining through the window. I was walking around on little sleep, and according to Google, Nash was going through a growth spurt.

Although I sympathized with him, and whatever pain he was experiencing, I wanted him to pity me. And my swollen eyes, my foggy brain, and the little energy I had to do something as simple as brushing my teeth.

But I needed more energy to walk him across the apartment, back and forth, because that was the only thing calming him, slightly. His screams were softer, and not as ear piercing. Then my legs grew tired, and I just had to take a seat. I was rocking Nash back and forth, when I heard my phone ring; it was mixed in between Nash's screams.

"Hello?" I said, trying to talk over the cries. "Nico?"

He had been home, but instead of him coming back to my apartment I suggested he stay at his place. I felt like I needed space. I thought I needed space. Even my mama got the boot, but Nash quickly taught me the error in my ways. "Is he okay?" Nico asked of Nash.

"Yes, well no, I don't know," I told him. "I think he is going through a growth spurt."

"You sound tired, Destiny, I should just come back."

I sighed. "Can you just come get him?" He repeated me, "Yes, come get him. Take him with you." Then I explained, "I just want to sleep."

"Should I call your mom?" he asked, and I quickly shot that idea down. "Are you sure you want me to keep him with me, like overnight?"

"Yes, you come get him and you take him to your place so that I can sleep. I have milk bottled for him," I told him in case his next excuse had to do with my boobs. "When will you be here?" I asked desperately.

"Give me twenty," he said before we hung up.

I looked down at Nash and told him, "Your daddy will be here soon." As if that's exactly what he needed to hear to calm down, his cries stopped and I said, "Did you just?" and tilted my head. "I can't believe this."

I walked around with him, as I gathered his diaper bag and stuffed it with diapers, clothes, and even a blanket. Then I went to the refrigerator and grabbed his bottles and a freezer pack. By the time Nico showed up, Nash was pretty much bundled up, sitting at the door waiting for him. "Come back tomorrow," I instructed.

"But," he hesitated, "I don't know what I'll do with him that long."

"I've been figuring it out." I blew Nash a kiss and told Nico, "you'll be fine."

Chapter Twenty-Seven

Nico

On the car ride to my apartment Nash fell asleep in the backseat. Atlanta had a lot of road to ride, and I was tempted to drive up and down all of it to keep him sleeping, but I realized that wasn't realistic. I would have to face him. I parked in front of my building and as I maneuvered his bag and his car seat, I made my way to my front door. With each noise, slammed door, or voice that was too loud, I cursed, "Fuck," under my breath, then I'd look down at Nash still sleep in his carrier. "This isn't too bad," I whispered, "I can do this."

Nash in his carrier wasn't the same Nash that entered the apartment. That Nash was the one I heard crying on the phone when I was talking to Destiny. That was the Nash that likely had his mama willing to hand him over to the least qualified person in her life. "C'mon, man." Then I looked at the TV. "How about we watch the game?" I hushed him and bounced him on my knee.

The buzzer rang for half-time, and I searched my pockets for my phone. As soon as Nova picked up, I shouted, "Put Harmony on the phone."

When she was on the phone, she asked, "What's wrong?"

"I need your help," I pleaded, and she laughed. "I'm serious. I had to take Nash so Destiny could sleep. We are at my apartment, and I don't know what to do."

"Feed him, Nico. Wash him up, then put him down to sleep." I scoffed as if it were that easy. "Why are you still on the phone? Go do that."

"Harmony, Harmony, wait. Please?" She told me no plainly, then when I asked, "Okay, put Nova back on the phone," she just laughed. "And I thought I liked her." Then I gambled, "How about you? Can you come over?"

"Me? Naw, man." He waited for Nash's cry to calm down. "I'm not the man for the job. But you know who you should have called?" When he said our mama, I wanted to hop through the phone and kiss him.

"Of course, yeah. Alright." I hung up with him and when she was on the phone, I asked nicely, "Mama, can you come to my apartment and help me with Nash?"

And in that moment, I knew she was the best person in the world. "I'd love to come over. I'll be there in a few."

By the time she had arrived I had given Nash a bottle and changed him into his pajamas. "Give me that baby," she said when she walked through the door, and I did gladly. "What is he doing to you?" she asked with her nose snuggled into his neck. He started cooing and calmed down. I flopped onto the couch and thanked her. "You don't have to thank me, I'm happy to help." She looked around. "But where is Destiny?"

I explained, "She needed a break, asked me to bring him here so she could sleep."

She smiled. "Bless her heart. It's a lot being a new mama." Then she scowled. "Still not sure why she kicked both you and her mama out."

"Exactly. I just don't understand."

My mama adjusted on the couch beside me, Nash just staring up at her. "You know, when I had your brother, I had a hard time those first few months." She looked at me. "They weren't big on diagnosing it back then, but now I recognize what it was, postpartum. Destiny may need to talk to someone to make sure she's okay." I nodded my head.

"I'll suggest it. I tried to get her mom to help, but she just told me it was me causing her to be grumpy and disregarded everything else I was telling her."

She hunched her shoulders. "She's protective, I get it. Soon enough you'll get it too." She looked down at Nash. "We all just want what's best for our kids."

I was already starting to understand. There wasn't anything I didn't want to do for Nash. "I'm thinking this is too much for her to keep doing alone, especially in that small apartment."

"And what are you going to do?"

I had been thinking about it while I was on the road. My place wasn't much bigger than hers, so that wasn't an option. Her place was too small and already had her complaining with the two of them sharing a space. "I want to buy a house. For us to live in together."

My mom's eyes widened as she looked at me. "I think that would be a lovely idea. Just make sure she's in the right headspace for that change, and that the two of you are good." She passed Nash to me. "I'll always be available when you need me, but I think you needed this eye-opening experience to see what it takes to raise a kid alone."

"Wait, you aren't leaving me, are you?"

She shook her head. "No, not now, but I'm not staying all night, so you and Nash better figure out how you need me while you have me." I laughed.

"He was crying like crazy with Destiny when she called me, then asleep in the car. As soon as we walked through the door he started wailing again." I looked over at her. "Then you arrive and he's a saint."

She smiled, then told me, "Kinda like tech support, I can't ever get my phone to work right. As soon as I walk into the Apple store, boom, it's working for them." She laughed. "There's only three things a kid needs most of the time—and that's to eat, to poop, or to sleep." But then she placed a finger out for Nash to clutch. "And then there's love. That anxiousness the two of you probably have from being new parents is making him uneasy. Relax a bit, and he may calm down." I kept that in mind.

"There's one more thing I wanted to talk to you about." That topic was even harder than managing his cry. "His heart." The smile she had faded. "They've run all the tests they can at his age. And see nothing, but," I paused, "there's always a chance that it can develop later in life."

She moved her finger from Nash's grip and placed her hand on my arm. "Nico, we know the signs to watch for, and I'm sure his pediatrician will ensure he monitors him for them. As will you and Destiny." Then she smiled. "And don't forget your brother developed HealthScare for this reason right here, so that nobody would receive a fatal diagnosis too late. Does Nova have what he needs to use it to monitor Nash?" I nodded my head. "Then he already has more than you and I did, and that's a blessing."

"Thanks, Mom." Nash was still quietly sitting on my lap, his eyelids looking heavy. "I think I should feed him again and see if he'll fall asleep."

"I think that's a good idea." She stood from the couch. "If you need anything don't hesitate to call me. But I think you have this under control." As she walked to the door, I followed behind her, going into the kitchen with Nash in my arms. "And Nico, I just want you to know, I'm so proud of you." I didn't know if I quite deserved the compliment, but I thanked her anyway.

I placed a kiss on the top of her head and she said, "Love you both," before leaving the two of us alone.

The bottle and a diaper change did it for him. He laid in the bassinet I had for him and was sound asleep. I searched for my phone and sent a text to Destiny.

Nico: I hope you were able to get some rest. Don't worry about Nash, he's good.
Nico: And Destiny, I love you.

I didn't expect her to respond back, I was hoping she was fast asleep. But my phone rang a few minutes later, her name flashing on my screen.

"Nico." She sounded refreshed. Rejuvenated almost. "I love you." Then she told me, "Thank you for picking up Nash. I didn't realize how much I needed to sleep." Then she laughed. "And how much I needed help." Then she corrected, "If I had to do this alone, I think I could have." She quickly added in, "But why make myself do all that?"

"Exactly." I dragged it out for extra emphasis. "We are here for you." Then I thought about her mama. As much as I could have bashed her, I remembered what my mama had just told me. "Although your mama can be a bit much, I think she only wants the best for you."

"I realize that now. Believe me, first thing tomorrow I'm

begging her forgiveness and asking her to come over and help when she can."

"Good." Then I said, "Is there anyone else you want to help you out, anyone else you want to ask forgiveness of for kicking to the curb?" I waited.

Destiny laughed. "Oh, that person deserves that tonight."

"Tonight?" I asked, my eyes narrowing.

"Yeah, I'm on my way." Then she explained, "You have two bedrooms, and well, there's something else besides sleep I've been missing."

"Who you telling?" She told me she'd be there in twenty, and I stood from the couch, moving Nash's stuff to one area of the room, quietly, of course. I couldn't wake him before the main event. Then I prayed, "God, if you love me, you will let Nash sleep for longer than his normal two hours. Please, Lord." I looked up and cocked my head. "Amen."

The Lord answered my prayers, because when Destiny arrived looking like a fucking prize, Nash was still asleep. I whispered, "C'mon," and pulled her to my bedroom. "I see you got your hair looking right, your clothes," I pointed to the clean sweater she was rocking, "and that smile." I leaned in and kissed her lips. But then I pulled her back by the shoulders and asked, "But did you sleep?" She nodded her head.

"It's amazing what just a couple of hours of uninterrupted sleep will do for me now."

"Well, after I fuck you back to sleep, don't worry about waking up till morning. I have enough milk for Nash, and I'll check in on him through the night."

She pulled me by the shirt and said, "I think that's sexier than any foreplay. Come here." She swiped her finger under the hem of my shorts, then my boxers, and went down to her knees. I watched the whole sight with amazement, but as her warm mouth wrapped around my dick, I had to bite down on my finger to keep the noise down.

There was not a single inch of my dick that she didn't try to take down her throat, and as she looked up with a mouthful of me, I needed her in other ways. I reached down and touched her shoulder. "As much as I would like to finish just like this," I warned, "I think our time is ticking, and I need *all of you*."

She groaned. "This will be something to get used to." I didn't ask her what she was referring to, I was too busy pulling off her sweater, and her leggings. Finding my way around her new body—softer, curvier.

I instructed her to lay on the bed, and I kissed her legs and moved quickly to her inner thighs, where I tasted what I'd been missing for a couple of months. "Shit," I mumbled after I came up for a breath, "I didn't think it was possible to miss it," I kissed her again, "this much." Then I devoured her, kissing and sucking, gliding my fingers through her moisture, until I felt her body respond, and I told her, "Not yet," before I climbed off the floor and grabbed a condom.

She snickered. "You know I'm on birth control, right?" I cocked my head to the side and waited. "Right, just our luck."

I climbed on top of the bed and between her legs, then told her, "Now in about two or three years, we'll try our luck again." As her mouth hung open, I kissed it, filling it with my tongue. I grabbed both of her hands and stretched her arms out wide as I entered her slowly, taking my time as she readjusted to having me there after months. Her moan let me know she was as pleased as I was for the comeback. I released her hands, and she wrapped them around my neck, and it took all my might to continue moving gently inside when my body wanted to speed things up.

I moved from on top of her and let her take the lead, and her hips gyrated slowly at first, then suddenly, she was moving like before and I watched her face twist and contort, before a smile came across her lips. Her hips slowed and she rested her head on my chest. She kept moving her hips until I felt myself release.

"I missed the shit out of you," I whispered in her ear as I kissed the top of her head.

She climbed off me and laid on my side, her arm tracing circles on my chest. "I missed you too, Nico." She yawned then told me, "I feel a few more hours of beautiful sleep will be the icing on this cake." I kissed her forehead and listened as her breathing stilled.

Then the silence in the apartment was replaced by wailing. I went to the bathroom, quickly cleaning myself before I made my way to the guest room where Nash had been asleep. "Alright, little man, I got you," I told him as I picked him up from the bassinet, and as soon as I did his crying stopped. I kissed his forehead and whispered, "We're going to stay quiet for Mommy, okay?" before walking out to the kitchen to grab a bottle for him.

The bottle was in his mouth, and as I made my way back to the guest room, he suckled while I held him. Maybe it was the sound of him feeding, or the quiet of the apartment finally that had me hard blinking my eyes. "Okay, man, if you are going to poop do it now, or you are going back to sleep," I told him with a weak smile.

His bottle was empty, and I laid him back in the bassinet. We did that routine a couple more times before the sun was up, and when he was fully awake I took him to see his mama. "Good morning," I said, walking into the bedroom. Destiny stretched her arms wide and sat up in the bed. "Mind if we join you?"

"Of course not." She patted the bed beside her.

We sat beside her, and she reached for Nash, but I shook my head. "You still have a few more hours to indulge." Her head went back, and she snatched her hands away. "Enjoy it while you can."

"I know better than to complain. I'll get my hugs in later." She laughed.

"This," I looked at Nash who was cooing up at me then to her, "is everything."

She licked her lips. "Is it?" I nodded my head.

"You know," I rested my head on the bed, "I had to call my mom to help last night."

"Are you serious?" I nodded my head.

"I completely understand how hard this has been on you. And," I paused as she adjusted on the bed, "I don't want you doing this alone."

Her eyes widened. "You're getting me a nanny?" The thought of a nanny never crossed my mind not even once. I laughed until Nash looked like he was about to start crying, and I cut that shit off real quick.

"I was thinking we should move in together, then you won't be doing it alone."

Her nose scrunched up. "And what would that mean for us?"

"It would mean that we take this relationship seriously. We enjoy being a family of three until it's time for us to become four, or five, six maybe."

"Whoa. You had me until you started counting numbers I'm not familiar with." We both laughed, quietly. "Honestly, though, I'd really like that. To move in with you, to have a relationship with you." She tightened her lips.

"C'mon, count to at least four."

"Have a family of four." Then she cocked her head. "That's as good as you're going to get right now."

I leaned over Nash and pulled his mama's face to mine,

kissing her passionately. "Next step is to figure out how we can," I wagged my head, "you know, with the little one in the room."

"Hold that thought." She disappeared out of my room and returned with Nash's bassinet. She reached for him, placing him gently in the bassinet. "Now Nash, be sweet for Mama." Then she looked at me and said, "I bet we can work on our timing." She wriggled her brows. "We just need a few minutes, Nash." She climbed into the bed, and I showed her just how efficient I could be.

Epilogue

Nico

Before I was diagnosed with my heart condition, I imagined a perfect life being something I watched on television. A basketball player doing his thing on the court for some professional team, leaving the arena in a fast car, speeding to meet up with a random woman. Essentially, a good life felt like ball, cars, and women.

Never did I think that kids were even in the picture for me, unless, of course, it was a kid lining up to get my autograph or take a picture with me after a game. But a kid of my own, nope. That was never in my dreams.

I had no idea how big of an impact fainting on the court that day in high school would have had on my life. It was a dream crusher for sure. But as I stood in the kitchen waiting for the food on the stove while my family laughed and talked, I realized that day didn't crush my dreams. It set me up for a future I wouldn't have gone after on my own. Guess it was my little nudge.

In some way, God needed to nudge me a few times—I hadn't realized how reckless I was being until the pregnancy scare. And thankfully, that was the only thing that came of fucking random women and living life on the edge as some sort of dare devil pushing it to the limits.

When I looked at Nash trying to wobble his way across the living room, my entire insides burst with the same sort of excitement I had when I weaved my bike in and out of the Atlanta traffic, or the thrill of meeting a new woman.

Then there was Destiny, the woman I was sleeping on all along. The woman who was my everything before I knew I needed anything. Life was far greater than what I could have imagined. "Bruh," I heard Nova's voice as I felt his hand on my shoulder, "think it's about time to flip those burgers before they are bricks." He laughed. "You good?"

I looked down at the burgers and told him, "I'm better than good. Hand me that pan." I pointed to the foil pan I had sitting on the counter.

"Good, otherwise I would have had to remind you what you got here." He looked out over the house. "Little man is a whole year old. Like, that shit happened so fast."

I smiled. "Yeah, it happens too fast." I flipped the burgers from the stove to the pan and advised, "Remember that when your little one gets here."

"I'm ready, man." Harmony was pregnant with their first child, and she, too, was wobbling around the house chasing kids around.

"Just know that if you call me one night in desperation, I'm not coming." We both laughed. The doorbell rang, and I told him, "Watch the rest of the food, I'll grab the door." When I pulled the front door open, the one person I wasn't extremely excited to see stood on the other side. "Ms. Harlow, come on in."

I moved aside and let her walk through, taking off her coat to hang it in the closet.

"Thank you, Nico," she said with a tight-lipped grin. "Where are my babies?"

I pointed to the back of the house. "Everyone is in the living room."

Before she moved, she told me, "Nico, before we get in front of everyone, I just want to tell you that I'm proud of what you and Destiny are doing." There was a slight smile coming to her face as she continued, "You two are doing great with Nash, this house." But then the smile faded, and she told me, "Only thing missing is a wedding to concrete your relationship."

I reached in my pocket, pulling out the box I planned to present to Destiny later that evening. "Oh, don't worry, I plan to make that happen soon enough." She gasped, her hand going to her mouth. "Yeah, sorry to let you know you're going to be stuck with me. I'm here for the long haul."

Her hand reached for mine and she said, "I honestly hope so, Nico."

I pulled her into a hug, surprising the both of us. "If it's up to me, this thing we're building will be forever."

I released our embrace, and the smile she had building on her face had returned. "And I'll be here cheering you on."

"Thank you." We walked through the house and when Nash saw her, he moved as fast as his little legs would allow. "Slow down, man, before you stumble over," I shouted. But that didn't stop him, he was on a mission.

After we all ate, Destiny helped rip the paper from Nash's gifts, and when the last was opened I announced, "Everyone ready for cake?" As the party winded down, I was walking around the house, picking up random plates, cups, and toys that Nash's dearest friends had thrown. But it was time to feed everyone cake so I could move on to the part of the party I was looking forward to. With our families and friends in the room, I thought it would be the perfect time to propose.

"Yes," Nova walked to the kitchen with me, "Let's eat cake," he said loudly before asking me in a soft voice, "you good?" He knew all about my plan, since he was there when I picked out the ring that was burning a hole in my pocket.

"Yeah, I'm good, I think I just need to get to it."

He nodded his head and helped me walk the cake out to Nash with a lit candle. I fumbled with my hands as we sung two renditions of "Happy Birthday," then watched anxiously as he blew out the candle.

"Let's cut it." I followed Destiny to the kitchen as she cut a hefty slice for him. "He has to smash it all over his face." Then she yelled, "Harmony, make sure you have the camera ready."

She sat the cake in front of him, and as he was busy stuffing cake in his face, I cleared my throat and tugged on her hand. Standing beside the two of them, I said, "Listen, everyone, I have one more thing I want to give Nash for his first birthday." I looked at Destiny and started the speech I had repeated in my head all day. "I think we can both agree that Nash is everything to the both of us." Destiny was smiling and nodding her head. "And in this year of his life, there is someone else I have realized means the world to me." Her eyebrows narrowed. "Destiny, I know our relationship hasn't been conventional, but there's not a single person in this world I would rather shake shit up with."

Her eyes widened as she reminded me, "Language, babe." And that's when I realized she was sniffling. Everyone laughed.

"Destiny, will you," I dropped to my knee realizing I was still standing, "marry me?"

She wrapped her arms around my neck and pulled my lips to hers. Behind us I heard, "Mama?"

I stood from my feet and looked at her. Repeating Nash, I said, "Mama, what's it going to be?"

"That's a hell yes!" And everyone cheered.

But I told her, "Language," and winked as I pulled her back into my arms.

☆☆☆☆☆

If you enjoyed this story, please leave a review on an eBook retailer, and blast me all over social media. Because as an indie author, I thrive off of reviews.

Thank you for the support!

Also by J. Nichole

Visit www.notthelastpage.com/books for a full list of books.

About the Author

J. Nichole is an HBCU graduate, a wife, and a Black mama. She is in love with love, especially Black Love.

For more information:
www.NotTheLastPage.com

Made in the USA
Middletown, DE
18 November 2023